Beat Bongni
Your Compass

A special thank you goes to the Inselspital Bern and
to my former colleagues at Swisscom: a great team!

Beat Bongni
**Your Compass**
Living by the Law of Attraction

Translated from German by ChatGPT

Printing and distribution: BoD — Books on Demand, Norderstedt

© Production and publishing: Publishing Partners, Switzerland
Editing, Co-author: Werner Affentranger
1st edition 2024
ISBN 978-3-907147-39-9
Cover: created by the publisher

Beat Bongni

# Your Compass

## Living by the Law of Attraction

Publishing Partners

# Inhalt

# Preface

One evening, Beat Bongni called me and asked if I would be interested in publishing his book. He gave me some information about its content, and I replied that he could send me a few pages of his manuscript. This is my usual response to such inquiries, and I always read the submitted samples before deciding whether to accept or decline.

Beat sent me a link to his manuscript, which spanned more than two hundred A4 pages. The sections were partly written recently and mostly years ago, with annotations and links to books by other authors or topics that interested him.

While skimming through, I realized that Beat had traveled extensively and mentioned many people known in Switzerland: personalities from politics, business, and sports, such as a former Federal Councilor, a Federal Councilor, well-known entrepreneurs, and people frequently seen on Swiss television. I was amazed that Beat had personal connections with all these people and still maintains friendly contact with many of them — Beat retired early a few years ago.

The first chapter of his manuscript began with a near-death experience, describing Beat's cardiac arrest on June 21, 2019. He survived thanks to incredible luck, the quick intervention of an acquaintance who had previously attended a first aid course and happened to be in the right place at the right time, and professional help from paramedics. This was followed by a two-month stay at the Inselspital in Bern, during which he spent the first three weeks in a coma.

Most of the manuscript pages were flashbacks to important events in Beat's life, notes, and travel reports, all arranged non-chronologically. It was undoubtedly an interesting and extraordinary life story, I thought. However, during our first meeting, when Beat handed me a stack of books by bestselling authors on partly spiritual and partly scientific topics, I realized that his book was not primarily about his biography. Beat had intuitively trusted his inner compass for major decisions in his life, and this compass is the main focus of his story.

As the child of a working-class family, he had dreams and visions of material prosperity and adventure travel. After completing his apprenticeship as a metal construction locksmith and technician, he began to realize his dreams, starting with an immigrant visa to Australia, where he sought his fortune as a gold and opal prospector. He returned to Switzerland, furthered his education in business, started a family with his childhood friend Lisa, and pursued a career that eventually led him to the executive suite as Director of Marketing and Sales at Switzerlands largest telecom company.

It would not do Beat justice to only highlight the successes of his professional career. Beat was and is a seeker who asked himself the big existential questions as a teenager: Where do I come from, where am I, where do I want to go? He searched for answers and embarked on a journey of self-discovery. He found his way to an evangelical church and, as a young adult, got baptized again with Lisa. This was meant to cleanse him of sin and confirm his integration into the Christian community. However, the church rituals did not convince him that he had found his destined path in life, and he left the evangelical church again.

While reading books by authors dealing with existential and religious questions, Beat came across two volumes by Neville Goddard: "Freedom for All" and "The Power of Awareness." According to Goddard, there is only one master, despite all the gods in some religions, and this master is God within me, within myself. This thesis opened a new way of thinking for Beat and doors he had not previously noticed or had considered closed. God and the kingdom of heaven do not wait for us somewhere, as church preachers proclaim; rather, everything is within us, waiting to be discovered.

Beat delved into Goddards theories on the law of attraction and found confirmation of what he had previously felt subconsciously: positive thinking brings positive results, while negative thinking drags you down. Beat is living proof that dreams can come true: he has achieved almost everything he once dreamed of. After suffering from a lack of oxygen in the brain as a result of cardiac arrest, he even found his way back to life without any lasting impairment of his cognitive abilities. This made Beat interesting for the neurologist and researcher Philipp Koch, whom he met during his stay at the Inselspital. Both realized that they could learn from each other.

Beat's manuscript could not simply be adopted, edited, and published as a book without first reorganizing everything, omitting repetitions, incorporating annotations, and turning notes into dialogues. During our third meeting, he handed me a thick stack of his personal resume, numerous photos, and newspaper clippings about him, along with many handwritten notes. It was an interesting collection of data, too valuable not to do something with.

I saw only one way to turn these diverse parts into a coherent book: the manuscript had to be rewritten. Beat immediately agreed when I offered him this option.

As a result, this book was created through a beautiful and exciting collaboration with Beat. I thank him for the trust he placed in me.

This edition was translated from German to English by ChatGPT. Native English readers have found the text to be accurate and encouraged us to publish it unchanged.

Werner Affentranger

*There are two types of deception:*
*One is to believe what is not true,*
*and the other, not to believe,*
*what is true.*

*Soren Kierkegaard (1813–1855)*


*Imagination is more important than knowledge,*
*Because knowledge is limited..*

*Albert Einstein (1879–1955)*

# Cardiac Arrest

On June 19, 2019, Beat Bongni sets off on a trip to Tenero. There, he plans to participate in the Swisscom Games. For the next three days, he will stay directly on Lake Maggiore, from where a bike path leads to Tenero. He looks forward to leaving his car parked at the hotel and traveling by bike. With this, he will be able to reach the grounds of the Federal Office of Sport, where the Swisscom Games are held, in just fifteen minutes.

He is eagerly anticipating the event the next day, in which around 5000 active Swisscom employees will participate in various disciplines. Beat is the team leader of one of the sports groups and will run the nine-kilometer jogging track himself. His colleagues will compete in mountain biking, cycling, and swimming. The start and finish for everyone is in Tenero.

Beat inputs Locarno as his destination in the GPS and checks the estimated travel time and any potential obstacles or traffic on the route. He trusts the pleasant female voice giving him instructions on the fastest way from Bern to Ticino.

During the drive, Beat's thoughts drift into an imaginative world without losing focus on the road. He imagines that humans also possess an internal navigation system and believes that this inner system has often guided him to the right place at the right time in his life. He likes the comparison. Yes, every decision we make is symbolically like entering a destination in the GPS. If you deviate from the route, you won't reach your goal in the desired time.

Beat's thoughts lead to a reflection on his 59 years as a citizen of the earth. He realizes that many of his life circumstances and everything around him are the result of his past decisions and goals. This thought fills him with great gratitude, as he is aware that he has never fallen into depression or suffered from burnout.

On his route to Ticino, he passes Wassen and approaches the entrance of the Gotthard road tunnel. The traffic has been smooth so far, and the friendly GPS voice has reported no obstacles. He lets his BMW glide along at 120 km/h using the cruise control. It's nice to be guided to the destination with ease, just as he is experiencing now. But what is ease, really? The word likely comes from letting go, allowing oneself to be guided. That seems to make sense, he thinks.

As he enters the tunnel, an unexpected thought crosses his mind: The investigation was only three months ago. His heart and physical fitness were subjected to various tests. Two days later he received the top result: above-average values for a 59-year-old. A healthy body, examined and found to be in top shape. That's how it should be, and this matter doesn't have to concern him now or in the next few years until he retires.

Only two kilometers to Airolo. He can already see the tunnel exit, that small white light growing larger. And soon, a bright blue sky greets him. The sun blinds him because his eyes have become accustomed to the darkness of the tunnel.


After another hour of driving, he parks his car at the hotel and checks into his room. Shortly after, he is already biking to the Swisscom Games grounds. He looks forward to checking in and meeting his colleagues soon. He received his race number for the next day after the team briefing in the large gymnasium. It is number 303, a nice number, he thinks.

Beat strolls towards the lake, passing numerous bars and food stands. The Swisscom Games are always a highlight, a huge festival. But he doesn,t want to linger too long; there will be plenty of time to celebrate with his colleagues after the sports events conclude. He wants to be fit for the race next morning along the Maggia and the lake. The route passes Monte Verità — the Ticino Mountain of Truth, where Hermann Hesse once lived for a short time. Hesse was a welcome guest at the Continental Park Hotel in Lugano, where some of his books are displayed, opened to the pages mentioning Ticino, along with a prominently visible bronze statue in the hotel lobby.

Beat,s thoughts return to the running route along the lake to the mouth of the Maggia, then towards Losone, past the golf course, and back to

Tenero. He feels buoyant and full of anticipation for the coming day. He falls into a dreamless sleep until the next morning.

Beat has no inkling that his run will abruptly end around noon near the golf course, where a tournament is also being held.

Well-rested and full of energy, he sets off the next morning and begins the jogging circuit. The weather couldn,t be better; brilliant sunshine brings out the lush vegetation along the route in its most beautiful colors. The landscape and nature in the Maggia delta always fascinate him anew. He quickly takes a few phone photos for his loved ones at home, then a final selfie on the long bridge over the Maggia in Losone. He sends the photos to his family.

One kilometer left to the golf course, where his golfing colleagues spot him and wave briefly, then past the golf restaurant. Now only the long, narrow asphalt road that branches off at hole 13 and leads back to the finish.

Here, at hole 13, where Beat's business friend Thomas is about to sink the golf ball, Beat unexpectedly collapses. His head hits the asphalt hard.

Beat is unconscious within seconds. Thomas Marfurt, who witnessed the situation from a short distance, immediately runs over to help Beat up. But it,s not possible; Beat collapses, having lost all control over his body.

Feeling for the carotid artery, Thomas realizes there is no pulse. Fortunately, Thomas has basic knowledge of first aid and immediately starts resuscitation attempts to bring Beat back to life. He breathes oxygen into Beat,s body, repeatedly.

Within minutes, a doctor is on the scene. It quickly becomes clear that the air rescue service (REGA) must be called. Within ten minutes, the police arrive, secure the area, and the helicopter lands. The defibrillator is quickly set up: shock — pause — shock — pause. No reaction, Beat does not return to life. Cardiac arrest!

# In a Coma

The paramedics continue the resuscitation. Beat can still receive a little oxygen, which reaches his brain.

Beat is flown to the hospital in Lugano, where three stents are implanted around his heart in the emergency room to keep his blood vessels open. He is unaware of all this. He sees and hears nothing and feels no pain. He is so close to death that he exists peacefully in darkness and harmony in a timeless dimension, without knowing where he is. He has no desire for anything, simply lying there with no sense of space and time.

**Near-Death Experience: What People Experience When They Die**
The question of what it is like to die occupies many people. A new study on near-death experiences might shed some light: researchers found that our brain remains active for some time even after the heart has stopped beating.

A tunnel with a bright light at the end, one's life flashing before one's eyes, or even out-of-body experiences: some people have been very close to death and have returned to life. Their memory of the moment when the heart stops beating fascinates and has preoccupied science for years. Behind this lies one of humanity's oldest questions: What do we experience when we die?

Phil Göbel: Excerpt from stern.de on Septem-ber 25, 2023.

**Between Life and Death**
The debate over whether near-death experiences are actually tempo-rary journeys to the afterlife is highly polarized. For those who explain the phenomenon with spiritual or religious approaches, these experiences can be proof of life after death, indicating that the spirit can separate from the body and continue to exist independently and endlessly. From a scientific perspective, however, body and mind are inseparably

united. Therefore, there must be rational explanations for near-death experiences, which can be described, for example, through biochemical or neurobiological mechanisms.

Stefan Nadile spoke to about thirty people who had a near-death expe-rience for his doctoral thesis. He did not attempt to frame the stories in a religious or scientific context. "I approached the stories neutrally and was particularly interested in the significance the near-death expe-rience had for those affected", says Nadile.

His findings differ significantly from the approach of the International Association of Near Death Studies (IANDS), which also has a Swiss section. IANDS believes that near-death experiences almost inevitably re-present a turning point in the lives of those affected, leading to deeper spiritual insights.

"Only a minority of my interviewees described the experience as a turning point", says Nadile. He did not hear about any "enlightenments" or encounters with figures or things that were unknown to the person be-fore the near-death experience. "For most respondents, the near-death experience triggered a return to previous values." The biographical component plays a crucial role in the subjective meaning of a near-death experience.

Excerpt from the Bieler Tagblatt, March 30, 2024

One of the most astonishing features of many near-death reports is the out-of-body perception. Therefore, they are often referred to as afterlife experiences. Beat's consciousness also left his body and encountered the afterlife, where he was completely unaware of the world and the hospital, existing in peace. Three weeks passed before Beat regained consciousness from the delirium, although during this time, he had been flown by helicopter from Losone to the emergency room of the hospital in Lugano, where he was connected to high-tech machines and had three stents implanted. A week later, he was transported to the emer-gency room of the Inselspital in Bern.

## Delirium, Dream Scenes

In his current state, Beat is far from being able to think clearly. His consciousness is as if switched off, but his brain continuously produces images and scenes that he cannot influence or stop at will.

In an imaginative scene like a short film, he finds himself in the Australian Outback, where he meets an older man who explains where and how to find gold. The master and mentor mentions that life is not just about wealth and power but about love, peace, happiness, and fulfilling one,s heartfelt wishes. That is why he himself is here in White Cliffs in New South Wales. "The compass of life is within you", says the master.

Beat thanks him and says, "I want to be wealthy, work in a large director's office, go on business trips and big journeys, build a beautiful house, start a family, and become an investor."

The master listens attentively, encouraging Beat to continue: "Then I want to write a book. About my life from a simple working-class family in Biel. The book should help people and show what is important in our earthly life and what can be achieved with the right mindset. We are only here on Earth with our bodies for a short time, then our eternal spirit returns to where it came from."

The wise master smiles and responds, "Beat, you are on a spiritual journey and have understood that life is not just about money and material things. But that does not mean you have to give up your dream."

Then again, silence, peace, and darkness. In the coma state, Beat cannot wake up and reflect on what he has dreamed. Otherwise, he would have immediately known that it was Peter Indermühle who appeared to him in the dream. Peter, whom he had met almost forty years ago in the Australian Outback.

Occasionally, images from Beat's dreams reappear, episodes from his past life, such as the scene more than forty years ago when he sat opposite Professor Marti. Beat had seriously considered studying theology at the University of Bern and was invited for an interview. But during the conversation, Beat felt that he could not pursue the path that Professor Marti was suggesting out of conviction. "I feel that I am not meant to be a theologian. I want to enter the business world, study business administration, marketing, and sales, and earn money. I want to travel the world and learn about other cultures."

The professor nodded.

"I see. If that is the case, then a career in busi-ness is probably the better choice for you. However, I would like to point out that the pursuit of money and power is not necessarily the key to happiness. It is important to choose a career that aligns with your values and interests and where you can fully utilize your skills and talents."

"I understand, Professor. But I think I can have both. I can choose a career that provides financial security and at the same time allows me to pursue my passions and interests."

"That may be", replied the professor. "But also consider that in business, it is often about maximizing profits and promoting growth at any cost, which is not always in line with ethical principles. So, if you work in business, you may have to deal with moral and ethical questions and fig-ure out how to work in an industry that aligns with your values."

"I understand", responded Beat. "I will always ask myself these questions and try to act according to ethical principles. I am grateful for your ad-vice."

"It has been a pleasure to point you in a possible direction", Professor Marti responded kindly. "I wish you all the best in your career and hope you always remember that success is not only defined by money and power but also by happiness, joy, and fulfillment in what you do."


## Visit from Lisa

Beat has now been in the Berner Inselspital for five days. The doctors are confident that he will survive. "That was close", says the heart surgeon to Lisa, who stands at Beat's bedside with a pale face. "Luckily, he is very fit for his age. Your husband has a good chance of coming back to the real world, but you need to give him time to find himself. At the moment, he dreams a lot, you can see it in his expressions, and they don't seem to be nightmares. That's a good sign; his brain is active."

Perhaps it was Lisa's presence that turned Beat's timeless imagination into a film scene again. He and his Lisa live in a farmhouse in Lyss, in the Hardern neighborhood above the town. They sit in the living room on the old stove bench, making plans for exploratory trips. They are a couple but not yet married. Lisa and Beat are frequently approached about this during church visits. Living in cohabitation is not allowed. Premarital sex is also not allowed. But because of their planned world trips, marriage, despite the church's opinion, is not an option for them for now.

In 1979, it finally happened. Lisa and Beat, still unmarried, set off on their first exploratory trip after completing their careers, traveling by ship from Ancona through the Corinth Canal to Haifa in the Holy Land of Israel. Beat sees them standing on Mount Sinai, Horeb, where Moses once received the Ten Commandments from God. And visiting the Mount of Olives, where Jesus, according to the Bible, ascended to heaven after the crucifixion on Golgotha.

Then the Dead Sea, where Lot's wife's pillar of salt supposedly still stands because she looked back at Sodom. Then the Red Sea, where Mo-ses led the people to the Promised Land through the parted waters after the exodus from Egypt.

These images pass by Beat as if they were real until silence and peace establish harmony again.


## Visit from Claudia and Conny

Beat's daughters, Claudia and Conny, greet their father, who lies motion-less but with open eyes in the hospital bed. He looks up at the ceiling and shows no reaction to their greeting, not even when Conny strokes his hand.

"Do you think Dad can hear us when we talk to him?" Conny asks her sister.

Claudia is puzzled and examines the thin tube connected to a device next to Beat's bed, ending with a probe under the bandage on his wrist. This apparently provides him with life-sustaining nutrients, she thinks. She would also like to know if her father can hear or even understand when spoken to. "I don't know, but we can ask the doctor", she says, just as a man in a white doctor's coat enters the room and greets the two women warmly. The man is at most forty, so not much older than I am, Claudia guesses.

"We unfortunately don't know for sure", the doctor answers the question. "But we've often found that patients can remember surprisingly well what they heard while they were unconscious after an operation. Your father is in a sort of medically induced coma. You may have heard the term..."

"Medically induced coma? Why?"

"It's used to monitor the heart and circulation. It's not a permanent state but a process with fluid transitions from minimal consciousness to waking up and returning to real life. Sometimes he moves and gestures without any apparent intention behind it."

"And you can control all that?", Claudia asks. "How long does this process take, and will our father be the same as before the cardiac arrest?"

"Those are good questions", the doctor says thoughtfully. "It may take days, perhaps weeks, until Mr. Bongni wakes up. Only then will we see what cognitive abilities your father still has. Memory loss is a common side effect after cardiac arrests, but with patience and therapeutic support, memory gaps can be filled over time."

## Another Dream

While Beat's daughters stand by his bed, he closes his eyes and sinks into another dream. He sees how he chose the family he wanted to be born into on Earth.

Paul-Ernst from Cordast in the Canton of Fribourg found a job as a janitor in the post office building at the train station in Biel. He is happy and starts his work in 1958. On a Saturday evening out in Biel, he meets Verena von Allmen from Beatenberg at the dance hall near the central square. They become friends and soon marry. On April 25, 1960, Beat is born in the Beaumont Hospital in Biel — an interesting life on Earth begins.

Another event appears on Beat's life screen... In the timeless fourth dimension where he exists without consciousness, he sees himself at a symposium with Swisscom's major customers. Before the gala dinner in Thun, guests and Swisscom managers board the ship in Interlaken. He sees Kurt Aeschbacher from Swiss Television announcing to the guests that they are about to experience something extraordinary.

Then he sees a car slowly driving into the water and swimming like a boat. He recognizes Frank Rinderknecht steering the vehicle and waving to the passengers on the ship. The guests laugh and applaud enthusiastically, then the image fades, and another appears. He sees Kurt Aeschbacher sitting opposite him and listening. "You know, I don't believe in the existence of God the Just and the Last Judgment", the man explains. "And you, do you believe in God?"

Beat doesn't know what to answer and remains silent.

"But sometimes I envy people who believe in God", the man continues. "They believe that the wicked go to hell, and those who have not sinned can live an eternal life as heavenly residents in the afterlife. Do you believe that too?"

Beat finds no words to answer. Instead, he now sees his father sitting across from him at the kitchen table, agreeing that there must be a paradisiacal heaven as described in the Bible, and that wicked people are punished after death and burn in hell. This annoys his mother, for whom the Old Testament consists of fairy tales, like the story of Santa Claus. Beat wants to protest but again cannot utter a sentence. "When you're older and wiser, my son", says the mother, "you will have a different opinion than your father."

Suddenly, the dream images disappear again. Darkness and oblivion spread.


"See how peaceful he looks?" Claudia says to her sister. "I think he's dreaming something nice."

# Finding His Way Back to Life

## Back to Consciousnes

Beat regains consciousness three weeks after arriving at the Berner Inselspital. He lies in a room in the Anna-Seiler-Haus, which belongs to the Insel group. He doesn't know where he is and believes he is dreaming. The room and the bed he lies in can't be real. Mechanically, he presses the button on the dangling cable. Two minutes later, a nurse stands before him and greets him.

"Hello, Mr. Bongni, welcome to the Anna-Seiler-Haus. I'm responsible for you, my name is Mrs. Müller. You called me, what can I do for you?"

Beat is amazed and asks hesitantly where and why he is here. It confuses him that speaking is difficult; he has to search for words and struggle to articulate them clearly.

Mrs. Müller explains: "You are here because you suffered a cardiac arrest in Ticino. First, you were in the emergency department in Lugano, then here at the Inselspital Bern emergency department, and now you are in the Anna-Seiler-Haus in the neurorehabilitation department."

Beat is astonished and initially can't comprehend what he hears. He examines the woman, who stands smiling kindly at his bedside. A doctor? Or a nurse? His thoughts whirl as he asks: "Why? What am I doing here?"

Mrs. Müller explains slowly and clearly: "Here are patients with head and brain injuries who have had a stroke, a brain tumor, or, like you, acute oxygen deficiency in the brain. Your brain had an oxygen deficiency due to cardiac arrest, and you survived because resuscitation, an emergency doctor, and then a rescue helicopter were there within ten minutes. You have lost a lot of learned things, and we are here to help you with what we call neurorehabilitation treatment to find your way back to life."

Beat is again surprised because he doesn't know what has happened in the last three weeks. The two days before the departure to Tenero, the drive to the hotel, and the jogging track at the Swisscom Games are erased from his memory. Struggling, he formulates questions that come to his mind:

"Where is my car? What happened? Where is my family? How long have I been here, and how long do I have to stay here?"

Mrs. Müller only answers the last question: "That can't be said precisely yet. First, you will work with the psychotherapists, then the physiotherapists will put together a gymnastics program for you. Additionally, your heart will be monitored daily by cardiologists. There will likely be another operation where bypasses will be placed. This will all take three to four months."

"Three to four months?" Beat tries to comprehend what has happened and why it will take months until he can leave this surreal environment. Could it be that I'm just dreaming all this, he asks himself, unsure.

"Then we will know if a return to work and a normal life is possible", Mrs. Müller continues. "Or if you can no longer work and will then be compensated and supported by the disability insurance. We have a disability insurance advisor here in the clinic who will contact you. There are some forms to fill out in cooperation with your employer. Swisscom has already reported a case manager for you to clarify all questions with the disability insurance, your health insurance, and retirement provision."

Oops, thinks Beat. The mention of his employer's name triggers something in him: Swisscom, his job in the management of the countrys largest telecom company! A clue! His brain begins to retrieve memories from the upper layers of his consciousness.

So I'm tied up here for a long time. Cardiac arrest, resuscitated — so I was clinically dead or almost dead — and jumped away from death. It slowly dawns on him that his life must have been hanging by a thread and that here and now he is not in a dream world, but in a bed in the Bern Inselspital and has, as if by a miracle, arrived back in the real world.

Though Beat is only partially aware of what Mrs. Müller had explained. He tries to picture the whole process but is overwhelmed and exhausted. Mrs. Müller leaves him with a friendly smile: "I'll come back tomorrow. Rest and gain strength."

Beat doesn't drift back into his dream world. He is busy processing the information he received from Ms. Müller. Psychotherapists and physiotherapists are supposed to get him upright again after he had already entered the afterlife with one foot. Yes, he thinks, I need your help to get out of here and find my compass again.

He looks at the photo of his daughters Claudia and Conny and his wife Lisa on the bedside table. Where are they now? Will they come to visit him? They should know where he is. But how could they know, he wonders. The sunlight falls on his face, and he closes his eyes. The weight of his worries is too much, and he drifts off into a restless sleep.


## Puzzle pieces and visions

Beat now has time to think, a lot of time. He trusts the hospital's experienced doctors to do everything they can to "restore" patients like him, and he has realized that it will be a long process to return to normal life. A broken leg would be easier, he thinks, because I would just have to concentrate on learning to walk again. But brain damage?

Mrs. Müller and a man he is seeing for the first time come into his room. "This is Professor Koch", she introduces her companion. "He is a neurologist and will come to see you more often now."

"I'm glad", Beat replies. The two men shake hands.

Professor Koch smiles kindly. "It's nice that you're available again. I am pleased to meet you. You are a very interesting case for us, not only because of the procedure on your heart, but also in terms of the functionality of your brain."

"I was just thinking about that", Beat replies. "Do I have brain damage? That would be terrible!"

"I wouldn't call it that", says the professor, grinning. "Your lovely daughters, who visited you during your coma phase, wanted to know from me whether you would be able to function as you used to when you were able to go home."

"Yes... and what did you tell them?"

"We can't answer that exactly yet, but you have a good chance of returning to work because your brain isn't injured. Due to a short-term lack of oxygen, certain brain cells have become inactive, so you'll probably have some memory lapses. But we can work on getting as much of what's in a kind of dormant state back on track as possible. We'll start training tomorrow."

That sounds good, thinks Beat, after Mrs. Müller and Mr. Koch have left the room.

*

The next morning, shortly after breakfast, Beat receives a visit from Professor Koch. The man is of average height, slim, wears glasses, and is in his early forties, Beat estimates.

"We'll start with simple exercises", explains the professor. "We'll go back as far as possible to your earliest memories, that is, to your childhood and youth. What memories do you have there? Just tell us!"

This is not how Beat imagined the "training." And is this supposed to be a simple exercise? He needs some time to collect himself. He closes his eyes and is amazed to see images appear on his imaginary screen. His mother tells him about his birth. "I was born on April 25, 1960 in the Beaumont Hospital in Biel. My mother, Verena from Beatenberg, gave me the name Beat."

Professor Koch takes notes and Beat continues. "I grew up in humble circumstances in Biel, went to school there and when I was fifteen I had a conversation with my father Paul-Ernst, who asked me what I wanted to be when I grew up. He told me that I had to be a teacher or a doctor if I wanted to be wealthy. But I didn't want to go to school any longer and I didn't want to be a doctor either. I imagined what doctors have to do. Operate, examine bodies, treat sick people and those who have had accidents in sterile rooms.

'I can't do that', I said. 'And I can't stand seeing people bleed.'

Neither of these professions was an option for me and, surprisingly, my father was very pleased about that."

Professor Koch smiles and writes something down. "Interesting", he says. "And then? What profession did you choose?"

"A few months later, my father came up with a new idea. He had worked as a facility manager - previously known simply as a caretaker — in the large business buildings of the Post and Telecom in Biel near the train station. He managed a small team and also had external customers for whom he carried out certain work and orders for the maintenance of buildings. Among them was a small mechanical workshop and a blacksmith's shop. He organized a trial apprenticeship for me there. I completed this trial apprenticeship and then agreed with my father and master to start a four-year apprenticeship. It wasn't my dream job, but because at the time I had no idea what else I could do apart from visions that seemed unrealistic to me, I successfully completed the apprenticeship as a metalworker and technician."

"What kind of visions did you have back then?"

"Oh, they were somehow blurry, far removed from the real environment that was familiar to me. During my apprenticeship I occasionally had to carry out repairs in large executive offices or install new security doors. I came into contact with people who worked in such offices and sometimes had short conversations with them."

Professor Koch looks up from his notepad and sees that his patient's thoughts are obviously elsewhere. "Go on, tell us."

"Yes, working in an office and completing important tasks seemed more interesting to me than my manual job, even though I did not have the commercial training required for employees with responsible tasks in an office."

Another area of work was wrought iron products, which I was often able to make and then install in villas. These were garden gates, window grilles to beautify the facade and to protect against burglars. I was amazed at how beautifully some people lived. I wanted to live like that with my family, which I didn't even have yet. Of course I knew that this would require a lot of money, which I didn't have. I imagined how it would feel to own a single-family home, have a lovely wife and children, and be the boss of a large company and be able to do business with important people."

"Well, visions are natural prerequisites for setting a goal. Some people manage to make their dreams come true", the professor notes.

*The power of imagination - the ability to imagine events that lie far in the future...*

Beat smiles. He has just realized that he has realized many of his dreams over time. He knows the power of imagination and knows from his own experience what you can achieve in life if you don't just have dreams, but believe in yourself and your own chances. Dreams don't just become reality if you just dream. He would like to talk to Professor Koch about this.

The doctor looks at him expectantly, and Beat has the feeling that the professor is not just listening out of habit, but is genuinely interested in what his patient is telling him. "That reminds me of an encounter from that time that I haven't forgotten..."

"Tell me about it!"

"When I was doing work in large executive offices and villas, I could sometimes overhear what was being discussed and planned. Once I heard an assistant arranging a business trip to America for her boss over the phone. Another time I saw one of these CEOs walking out of the building in a smart suit and with a rolling suitcase. I spontaneously asked the secretary where the boss was going. I stood at the door, putting a new lock on it, and the woman looked at me in surprise. Mr. Mosimann had to go to a meeting in Paris today and wouldn't be back for another three days, she said.

I said that I would also prefer to go on such trips.

The woman did not seem to have taken my comment as a joke, but rather sensed the great longing I radiated to travel. In a conversational tone, she said: 'Yes, traveling broadens your horizons. I have a brother who worked for an aid organization in Africa for five years. There, in Malawi, he found a wife and married her. They later traveled to Australia and stayed there.'

I wanted to know, what is he doing in Australia."

She said she didn't know exactly. In his last letter he had written that he was looking for opals and was living in the outback with his family.

I was impressed and said that I could imagine going on an adventure trip like that. Then, to my surprise, the woman said that she could give me her brother's address. Her name was Erika, by the way, and she wanted to know my name.

Great, Beat. I'll write down Peter's address here for you in case you ever visit Australia, she told me.

"Exciting story!", says Professor Koch. "Can I guess? You later visited this Peter, didn't you?"

"You're right. But first I wanted to finish my apprenticeship, then do the evening technical college, and to prepare for that I took a course in electrical engineering. But Peter's address has stuck in my mind to this day: Peter Indermühle, Opalfields White Cliffs in New South Wales, Australia. He didn't have a telephone because the mines are more than a hundred kilometers away from normal civilization."

"It's amazing what you can bring out of your memory", praises Professor Koch. "You've got a full schedule now with gymnastics, cardiology examinations and so on, but I'd like to continue talking to you. I'll come back in a week."

"With pleasure." Beat is looking forward to the next meeting with Professor Koch. What is his aim when he asks me to tell him about my life, starting with memories of my childhood and youth? He probably just wants to find out whether I can still remember the most important events in my life so far. Like puzzle pieces that create a complete picture when you put them together correctly.

*

The following night, Beat actually travels to Australia in his dream, experiencing in brief how he flew to Down Under with the immigration visa in his pocket — which he had quickly obtained at the embassy in Bern because Australia needed professionals and he was welcome as a "metal construction technician".

Unfortunately without Lisa, his girlfriend at the time and now wife, who didn't want to give up her new job at Coop Lyss.

The scene changes suddenly and master craftsman Germann speaks to Beat. He encourages him to think about the ideal life. Beat is irritated by the fact that Germann, a wealthy businessman, lives in a four-room rented apartment with a complicated wife. He is, after all, an entrepreneur and owner of Metallbau AG.

Beat wakes up and remembers what he just dreamed. Yes, old Germann. He was a good man, and at the time I thought he was a miser, who was under the thumb of his strict wife at home. But that wasn't the case, the two were a happy couple and led a fulfilling life. Today I know that happiness and fulfillment in life are not based exclusively on wealth, he thinks. And if you're wealthy, you shouldn't show off. That's not how you win real friends.

Beat has met quite a few people in his life who were unhappy despite their material wealth.

## Lisa

Beat's dream scenes feel like fragments randomly tumbling around in his brain. His loved ones can help fill the gaps in his memory, and his colleagues will also be important to help him get back on track, he thinks.

With each passing minute since Beat returned to life with conscious awareness, the thought of Lisa, his wife, becomes more dominant. She is more important to him than anything else. More important than returning to work. His Lisa. Slowly, memories of their first meeting come back to him.

While searching for a partner, he met Lisa at a dance in November 1978 in Lyss. She was his first true love and had a heart of gold. From then on, they spent every free minute together.

Beat made plans for worldwide adventures. Exploring the Amazon in Brazil by inflatable boat, traveling to Nepal. Lisa wasn't enthusiastic about this because she was very content with life in Switzerland and didn't feel the urge to discover the big wide world.

In the years 1977/78, Beat often went out with Heinz Binggeli, a school friend. They knew the entertainment program in Biel's discos and restaurant meeting points. But they were looking for something new outside of Biel. So, Beat and Heinz ended up in the dance hall *Rössli* in Lyss, where "The Frogs" played.

There was a different culture here than in urban Biel. Men looked around and went to the table where a woman was waiting for a dance invitation. So Beat went to the table where Lisa was sitting. She didn't reject him and followed him to the dance floor. Afterwards, they got to know each other a little through conversation. Lisa lived in Hardern above Lyss, Beat in urban Biel.

Whenever such a Saturday evening ended, it was customary for friends who went out together to invite each other for a nightcap at home. Beat also went with a small group and Lisa to her home in Hardern. At three in the morning, everyone went home, and Beat returned to Biel. The next Sunday morning, he noticed that he had left his scarf at Lisa's.

That was a good reason to drive back to Hardern with the red Mazda. The greeting at Lisa's and her mother's was warm, and Beat was spontaneously invited to lunch. Lisa's mother made great efforts to pamper Beat with delicious food.

The spark of love between Lisa and Beat could easily ignite. Thanks to the forgotten scarf, Beat was often invited back, and soon he was allowed to stay overnight.

Only Hans, Lisa's father, was somewhat suspicious of whether something could come of the city boy with torn jeans and his beloved youngest daughter. Hans was skeptical. He was from Emmental, Schangnau/Bumbach, and had experienced the hard side of life as a contract child. He was able to leave that behind as an adult with the move to Seeland, Lyss, and the founding of a company for wall and floor coverings.

An old hit by Udo Jürgens comes to Beat's mind: *"I've never been to New York and never to Hawaii. I've never walked through San Francisco in torn jeans..."*

Torn jeans became a trend, and back then I was something of a trendsetter, Beat thinks amusedly.


## The Power of Positive Thinking

In the following days and weeks, time flies for Beat. Medical examinations, physiotherapy, and visits from his relatives, friends, acquaintances, and colleagues leave him little opportunity for meditation and sinking into dream worlds.

The physiotherapy quickly shows results. Beat moves confidently up the stairs to the rooftop terrace, where he enjoys the view over the city and the Gurten, Bern's local mountain.

The visits from Lisa and the children have helped Beat the most in finding his identity again. The conversations with them gave him the orientation he had been seeking in the first days after waking up from the coma.

But a large part of the journey back to his familiar environment still lies ahead. Another operation is pending, where two bypasses need to be inserted to stabilize narrowed coronary arteries, as Mrs. Müller explained to him. Beat is determined to follow all therapies and looks forward to the next operation with positive expectations.

*

Tarzi, once a Key Account Manager in Beat's team, visits him. Beat is grateful to be able to exchange thoughts with his friend of the same age. Together they used to go on hikes, often with their wives, and attended events that interested them.

"It's great to see you", Tarzi greets him with a broad grin. "But I wish it were under better circumstances. I heard what happened and I'm really worried about you."

"Thanks, Tarzi. It was quite an intense experience. I was in Tenero at the Swisscom Games when I suddenly had this cardiac arrest. It was like time stood still. Luckily, Thomas Marfurt was nearby and immediately called the emergency doctor. I can only remember fragments of those moments before I fell into a coma. Now I'm trying to get everything back on track and have to prepare for another surgery. For being alive, I can only be grateful."

"I can imagine what that must have been like. It's really frightening, considering how fit you were and never had any problems with your heart. But you look much better than I expected, Beat."

"Thanks, Tarzi. The first surgery went well, and the doctors here are really good. I feel like I'm in the best hands in this clinic. But lately I've been thinking a lot about my life, about its meaning and about what's really important and what's not so important."

"That sounds like a profound experience. Have you thought about whether you want to return to work? The business is going well at the moment."

"Yes, I've thought a lot about it. I love my job, but this experience opened my eyes. I've been thinking for a long time whether it's time to slow down a bit. As exciting as my job is, it also takes a lot of my energy. The idea of early retirement is becoming more and more appealing to me. I want to enjoy life more while I still can and spend as much time as possible with my family."

"That sounds like a wise decision. Life is too short not to enjoy it to the fullest as long as possible. Have you already thought about what you want to do in retirement?"

Beat doesn't have to think long: "I want to travel, spend more time in nature, and pursue my personal interests. I plan to write a book and maybe even give some seminars on personal development. I think it's time to follow my inner compass."

Tarzi nods appreciatively: "That sounds like a solid plan, one you probably already have in mind. I believe it's a good decision. Life should be lived and enjoyed, and you have a second chance. Use it to do what truly makes you happy."

After Tarzi says goodbye, Beat picks up the book his friend brought him as a gift: The Power of Positive Thinking, a worldwide bestseller from the 90s by Norman Vincent Peale (first published in the USA in 1952).

Beat smiles and is grateful for the conversation with his old friend. It was a moment of reflection and rethinking, reminding him to redefine the meaning of his life and choose the path that truly suits him.

*With hope and confidence, any problem can be solved.*

Believing that hope and confidence can solve all problems is a beautiful thought, Beat thinks; at least it's a good way to approach a difficult task. He resolves to read this book and many others that deal with the questions of the meaning of life.

# Phil

The second operation was successfully performed by Ophélie Loup, who worked at Bern's Inselspital with the internationally known Thierry Carrel. Beat coped remarkably well with the procedure, in which two bypasses were inserted. He particularly enjoys the subsequent collaboration with sports therapist Lüthi. In addition to physiotherapy exercises such as swimming and gymnastics, they take time for table tennis, badminton, and regular walks in the park of the Inselspital. After just one and a half months, the first half of the entire rehabilitation period, Lüthi remarked that he would soon run out of new ideas to challenge Beat.

Beat also showed himself willing to do all the exercises outside of the physiotherapy measures. He was tasked by his psychotherapist to buy everything needed to make muffin batter and then bake them. He did this with flying colors, and the muffins tasted good. He could also do small gardening tasks and enjoy tending to herbs and flowers.

Now he sits in his room reading the book about the power of positive thinking when someone knocks on the door and enters the room without waiting for a response. Beat looks up from his book and greets the visitor. "Hello, Professor. I didn't expect you today."

"Sorry for barging in like this, but I was nearby and wanted to take the opportunity to see how you're doing. I see you're reading an interesting book. Positive thinking, that's nice. An interesting book, I read it myself a few years ago. By the way, we've known each other for a while now, and I suggest we drop formalities. My name is Philipp, but friends call me Phil."

"Oh, I'm glad, Phil." Beat nods, smiling. "But our acquaintance has been quite one-sided so far. You know a lot about me, but I only know that you are a professor and neurologist."

"You're right, that's how it is with patients in our and other hospitals as well. Our contact with patients mainly involves medical clarifications and treatments. I'm a neuroscientist and work at the Inselspital in brain research. I'm interested in people like you, whose brains weren't sufficiently supplied with oxygen for a short time after an accident or cardiac arrest. Some of these patients suffer permanent damage, lose cognitive abilities, and can no longer fulfill their previous roles in society. You seem to be the rare exception, which makes you particularly interesting to me."

Beat puts the book aside and looks attentively at Philipp Koch. "What do you mean by that?"

"Don't worry!" Phil replies with a smile.

"Everything is fine with you. It's just that the results of your medical examinations and tests have puzzled me and my colleagues. We conducted extensive tests, and so far, all the findings are within the normal range. With you, the results seem better than normal, especially for a person your age who went through what you experienced. That's remarkable. It means you've recovered faster than expected, both physically and mentally. You're even showing a higher level of cognitive performance than before your cardiac arrest."

Beat listens attentively, impressed by the professor's words. "So you're saying that I've recovered better than most patients and that my brain function has even improved?"

"Yes, exactly", Phil confirms. "We are always interested in understanding why certain patients recover better than others and what factors contribute to it. Your case is of great interest to us because you seem to have particularly strong resilience and mental strength."

Beat nods thoughtfully. "It's good to hear that my recovery is progressing so well. But I'm also curious to know what makes me so unique in this regard."

"We're trying to find that out", Phil explains. "It could be related to your positive attitude and mental strength. Maybe you've developed special strategies over the years that have helped you overcome challenges and stress. We want to understand what exactly these factors are so that we can help other patients benefit from your experiences."

"I'm happy to share my experiences with you", Beat replies. "I've always tried to see the positive side of things and not let myself be dragged down by difficulties. Maybe this way of thinking has actually helped me in my recovery."

Phil smiles appreciatively. "That sounds like a very plausible explanation. Thank you for your willingness to work with us. Together, we can possibly find valuable insights that can help other patients."

Beat feels a wave of gratitude and hope rising within him. He realizes that his recovery is not only a personal success but also a potential contribution to science and the well-being of other people.

"I'm grateful for this opportunity", he says with determination. "If I can help make a difference, I will gladly do so."

Phil nods approvingly. "You are already making a difference, Beat. Your story is inspiring, and your willingness to share your experiences is invaluable. We will continue to work closely with you and learn from your journey to help other patients."

After the enlightening conversation with Phil, Beat feels a deep sense of purpose. He knows that his recovery is more than just a personal achievement; it is a chance to make a positive impact on the lives of others. With newfound motivation and a strengthened resolve, he looks forward to the future, determined to embrace every moment and make the most of his second chance at life.

# Flashbacks

During his remaining time at Inselspital, Beat pores over photo albums, collected documents, agendas, and diary entries that Lisa has brought him. He uses this time to set new goals and manifest them.

*"How do you write a book? How do you start?"*

Now that a new chapter in his life is beginning, he wants to realign his compass. Beat does this the same way he always has when he needed to reorient himself. He asks himself: Where do I come from? Where am I now? Where do I want to go?


## Memories of Youth

In the next conversation with Phil, which has taken on an almost friendly tone, the neurologist wants to know how he remembers growing up.

"Teenagers often behave carefree and rarely have a clear goal of what role they want to play in society. They are ready for all kinds of nonsense and want to try everything. How was it for you? Were you the exception?"

"I don't know what you're getting at", laughs Beat. "You might think I always knew what I wanted or didn't want, what I could or couldn't do. That's partly true. My colleagues from trade school would probably confirm that I was always very confident in my athletic abilities."

"Do you have an example?"


## The Bet

"Because of my well-trained body and the optimism I exuded, I was often challenged. Whether I could run the 45-kilometer distance around Lake Biel in less than four hours, swim nonstop from Biel to Petersinsel, and so on. Then one of the colleagues made a spontaneous suggestion, a bet: to carry Paul, one of our colleagues, up to the fifteenth floor of the high-rise building in Stadtpark without stopping."

"Pretty crazy. And I guess you accepted the bet", grins Phil.

Beat shakes his head. "Not immediately. I had to think about whether I could do it. Then I agreed, but only on the condition that I would get five francs from each of the twelve colleagues if I succeeded. After some discussion, the bet was on.

They were convinced they would win and six of them went up to the rooftop terrace to enjoy the view from Weissenstein to Chasseral and the lake. The others were to follow me and check that I carried Paul without stopping all the way to the roof above the fifteenth floor."

"I believe you were already sure you'd win the bet", Phil notes.

"I had never done anything comparable, but yes, I was confident."

"An example of your positive thinking. And of course, you succeeded; otherwise, you wouldn't have mentioned the story", says Phil, smiling.

"You're probably right. People prefer to remember successes over failures. So, while I climbed step by step with Paul on my back, the colleagues behind me had philosophical conversations. Diego, the intellectual among us, quoted Jean-Jacques Rousseau:

*'Youth is the time to learn wisdom. Old age is the time to practice it.'*

Diego was the only one who believed I could win the bet. After the sixth floor, I was panting like a steam engine because Paul had both arms around my neck and my legs were getting heavier. But after the tenth floor, I felt a surge of energy. On the top steps, I quickened my pace, stepped onto the rooftop with Paul on my back, and received the applause from my colleagues."

"Really crazy", Phil remarks. Then he changes the subject: "And how was it with girls back then, for example with your Lisa? Was that your first love?"

**First Love**

Beat looks thoughtfully at the ceiling of the cafeteria, their meeting place in Inselspital. "Well, there was Lara first", he answers hesitantly.

"And? Tell me!"

"Lara was the woman who pretty much matched my ideal, at least physically. After nearly two years, she chose another partner and left me just like that. At first, it was a big disappointment for me, but I learned that for a lasting relationship, other qualities of both partners are more important than dream images we have.

That led to my desire to have a lifelong partner. Much later, by chance, I found out that Lara died of a serious illness ten years after our separation. It might sound cynical now, but I must be grateful to fate for sparing me from standing suddenly without family and purpose. My life would have turned out completely differently. Lara was my first crush, my first experience of love. But Lisa was my first real love."

Beat then tells Phil how he met Lisa and how their lasting relationship developed.

"I believe you have a harmonious relationship", Phil says. "That makes me happy. And at some point, you got married and started a family. Would you like to tell me how things continued?"

"Gladly, but give me some time, because a lot happened before our wedding: graduation, further education, military service, a four-month stay with Lisa in Israel, and then my emigration to Australia. I need to look through my records to see what I still have from that time."

"That sounds very exciting. I didn't know you emigrated to Australia. You must tell me about these events at our next session!"

Beat plans to gather everything he documented in the '70s and '80s for Phil. He thinks some of it could also be useful for the book he wants to write.

**First Trip Abroad with Lisa**

At eighteen, Beat passed the driving test for cars and 125cc motorcycles. He saw owning a car as an absolute necessity to feel free and be able to go anywhere anytime.

With his first vehicle, a red Mazda he bought as a cheap occasion, he and Lisa traveled over the Route Napoléon to southern France and made a stop in the Camargue to experience a horseback tour in the sand. It was a new experience for Beat and Lisa, but it wasn't enough to make them passionate about riding. They were more tempted to go to the Côte d'Azur and see the places where the rich and famous live.

In Cannes, Monaco, Nice, and St. Tropez, they got a glimpse of the luxury that only the super-rich can afford by visiting the mansions, villas, and yacht harbors.

Since childhood, Beat had felt that he had the ability to imagine what he wanted to be in his life. Pictures, books, adventure films, and beautiful houses inspired him to see himself in the future.

*Here you see for real what you have dreamed of so far. But is it really what you want?*

Beat was impressed but not particularly surprised by the status symbols of wealth that could be seen here. They had parked their Mazda next to a Bentley, in which a chauffeur sat waiting for his boss.

"Bonjour monsieur", Beat had called to him. The man responded with a tired nod.

Terms like "money aristocracy", "oligarchy", and "tax havens" were foreign to Beat at the time, but he guessed that an ordinary wage earner could never afford to live here.

They went to a nice-looking café at the yacht harbor in St. Tropez and ordered coffee and croissants. The waiter took the order without a word and brought what they wanted and the bill a few minutes later, just as silently. Beat looked at the note twice and thought the waiter must have made a mistake: 96 francs, which was about thirty Swiss francs! He put a hundred francs on the table before they left the place in silence.

On the way back to the car, he casually remarked to Lisa, "Come on, let's drive across the border to Italy."

Driving along the Ligurian coast with a stopover in Sanremo, they reached San Bartolomeo al Mare, where they found a lovely hotel right by the sea. The reception was friendly, the room inexpensive, and the dinner in a nearby pizzeria was just to their liking. The waiter was delighted by the visit of the giovani svizzeri and complimented Beat on his companion: "È una bella donna."

What a difference, thought Beat. There, the filthy rich snobs, here, this joy of life.


**First Trip to Israel**

When Lisa and Beat first traveled to Israel in 1979 — still unmarried — and worked for three months in Kibbutz Kfar Giladi in the north of the country, near the border with Lebanon, they found that the Israelis in the Holy Land think and live very differently from Christians in Switzerland. Their faith was different, and above all, it was always about the existential question of Israel. The country is surrounded by states that do not recognize Israel as a nation.

They found the orthodox Jews, who adhere to the traditional teachings written down in the Torah and Talmud, to be foreign and strictly devout. Lisa and Beat took the opportunity to visit Jerusalem and were amazed by the rabbis who prayed at the Western Wall three times a day.

"They live their lives according to the Halacha", explained the guide of a tourist group that Lisa and Beat had joined. "The Halacha contains more than 600 commandments and prohibitions, whose interpretation is set out in the Talmud and the Torah and is interpreted by the rabbis. Ancient Jewish laws and traditions are fundamentally preserved, but the rabbis often disagree on how to interpret the rules of conduct and often engage in disputes among themselves."

Beat was astonished and wanted to know if the clothing of the Orthodox Jews was also prescribed and if there could be disputes about that. He realized that it was a naive or perhaps even provocative question, but he waited eagerly for the answer.

"No, there are no disputes about that", said the tour guide. "Almost all devout Jews wear a head covering out of respect for God, the kippa, and ultra-Orthodox men wear a hat over it. Orthodox Jewish women wear a modest long skirt and a headscarf in public.

The disputes are not what you might think, but rather theological discussions and interpretations of the sacred texts", he continued. "The Talmud contains all sorts of instructions for everyday life, from food to family life. But some of these rules are thousands of years old, and sometimes it is not easy to apply them to modern life. For example, the question of whether electric lights can be turned on during Shabbat or if a kosher phone can be used. These are the kinds of things rabbis debate."

Beat was amazed at how religion could so deeply influence and even dictate daily life. He pondered how his own faith, which seemed so simple in comparison, could compare to this profound devotion.

On the way back to the kibbutz, Beat and Lisa discussed their impressions of Jerusalem, the Western Wall, and the devout lives of the Orthodox Jews. They marveled at how different their experience in Israel was compared to their life in Switzerland. They both felt that this journey had opened their eyes to a new world and gave them a greater appreciation for the diversity of faith and tradition.

Lisa smiled and said, "You know, Beat, I think this trip has taught us not only about Israel and its people but also about ourselves and what we believe in."

Beat nodded. "Yes, it's true. It has been a journey of discovery in more ways than one."

After four months in the Middle East, Beat and Lisa longed for peace and home again. The end of their trip was Cairo, where they booked a cheap flight. They flew back to Switzerland with what was then called Swissair.

Her goal now was to earn money and save money so that she could go on a trip again soon. Beat found a temporary job as a metalworker.

## Beat didn't want to join the military

Like all young Swiss men, Beat received an invitation from the army at the age of eighteen to be drafted to recruit school. The letter told him that he could state his preference for his assignment, such as grenadier, tank soldier or infantryman. If he had a medical certificate about a physical complaint, he should present this at the draft.

Four months of basic training was not what he wanted at all. It would completely mess up his plans for future trips and professional training. He was athletic and healthy, but he didn't want to join the military. Were there alternatives? If so, what were they?

Beat was against war, violence and the military. He had learned from all the books of wisdom and understood that violence was not compatible with a peaceful life. Should he refuse military service? He would have to submit a request and, if this was accepted, he would have to do community service, which lasted half as long as military service. That was out of the question for him. But if he refused community service too, the military court could sentence him to prison.

Should he emigrate? Beat began to think seriously about this idea. He remembered Erika, who had told him about her brother Peter Indermühle , who was looking for gold and opals in Australia. It was a tempting idea, but he would have to prepare carefully for emigrating. It couldn't be done overnight.

Another way to avoid compulsory military service would be to get a doctor's certificate stating that you are physically unable to perform your duties. Wait a minute, thought Beat, I sometimes feel a stabbing pain in my back, especially when I'm cycling or swimming!

He decided to have an examination. The results after a week were interesting. Beat was healthy and fit, but the X-rays had revealed a curvature in his spine, a so-called Scheuermann spine disease. The doctor explained to him in detail what "Scheuermann's disease" is and that this growth disorder of the spine could result in lifelong back pain.

"Wonderful!" Beat almost exclaimed. Instead he said to the doctor: "I have to go to the draft for recruit school soon. Can you give me a certificate of physical disability?"

The growth disorder visible on the X-rays gave Beat hope when he was drafted. But the doctors and recruiting officers did not consider him completely unfit for service. He was assigned to the post of a capable office orderly. He did not have to complete recruit school, which Beat considered at least a partial success.

When he was called up for a mission in Romont in western Switzerland, he enlisted. Instead of a weapon, he was given a mechanical typewriter, and instead of training to operate an assault rifle, he had to practice touch typing. Regardless, he had imagined his professional future in the office world anyway and considered his contribution to national defense to be an absolute stroke of luck.

While the soldiers of the infantry company, fully equipped, crawled around in the cold on the battlefield under barbed wire, urged on by loudly shouting non-commissioned officers, he wrote daily orders on the typewriter in the warm command office, which he then had to post wherever the soldiers were to take note of them.

In the command office, Beat was able to see how the army leads and gives orders, and he compared the military leadership style with the one he had previously experienced in the private sector. It was an interesting discovery for him that rank plays a decisive role in the military. Orders are given strictly from top to bottom, and orders must be followed unconditionally. The following applies particularly to the lowest ranks: receive orders and carry them out exactly, do not think about them or even ask why. As a sign that he has understood the instruction, the lowest-ranking person, i.e. the recruit or soldier, must stand at attention, clearly state that he has understood, and repeat the order. Poor or incorrect execution of an order causes the superior to shout and usually results in punishment. Rank also played a role among the officers, but Beat noticed that they treated each other with much more respect, often even in a friendly manner.

While Beat was taking a short break, an officer spoke to him: "How do you like it here?"

"It's fine", replied Beat. "But I'd actually rather be in southern Italy right now. I had to postpone the trip because of my military service."

"You like to travel? You can do that with us too. There will be troop movements next week", grinned the lieutenant.

Beat explained that he was slowly getting used to the military tone of conversation, but that he still had to get used to it.

"You'll have to get used to it", said the lieutenant. "Consider military service as training for an emergency, that is, for a possible state of war. Decisions can no longer be discussed and made democratically. Discipline and obedience are then absolutely crucial. And most soldiers are happy when orders are given clearly and they then know what to do."

Beat remembered this conversation. It made sense to him that different rules and laws would apply in a state of emergency. He was happy to have mastered his first military deployment passably. And indeed, he sometimes felt slight back pain after sitting for hours at a desk with the typewriter in front of him.

Many years later, as a key account manager and sales director for the federal government and the army, Beat had direct contact with senior officers, divisional officers and the CdA (Chief of the Army) at Swisscom. He was even able to organize top-level meetings and attend himself when Carsten Schloter , then CEO of Swisscom, met with Ueli Maurer, who was head of the Ministry of National Defense as a Federal Councilor. At the level of divisional officers, brigadiers and colonels in the General Staff, everything was less formal and Beat was soon on first-name terms with many of these officers.

*

"You're a real surprise package", says Phil. He and Beat are sitting at their regular table in the cafeteria. Beat has found what he was looking for in his diary entries and documents over the last few days and was able to give Phil the material and add to it by commenting on it.

"I see that you have enough material to write a book. And when are you going to tell me about your emigration to Australia?" Phil wants to know. "There was this Peter who was looking for gold and opals in Australia and who you wanted to visit."

"You have a good memory", acknowledges Beat. "In fact, Peter Indermühle was the trigger for this trip. I can tell you how it went the day after tomorrow, at our next meeting."

*

Beat is gradually beginning to prepare himself mentally for his return to work. He has received regular visits from his colleagues, who were pleased with his physical progress. It seemed clear to them that Beat would soon be returning to work.

Beat sees things a little differently. He is grateful that he will soon be able to return to his job and the responsibilities that come with it. However, the cardiac arrest and the last few weeks in the hospital have had a noticeable impact on his inner compass. He feels that professional challenges no longer hold the same attraction for him as they did before his cardiac arrest.

## First Trip to Australia

Phil is clearly looking forward to Beat's emigration story. Beat has made only a few notes and explains to the professor that he can tell him everything off the cuff.

"Australia at that time, in 1980, was a country of immigrants. As a metal construction technician, I was welcome and got a visa. However, after arriving, I didn't look for a job right away but first visited my schoolmate Heinz Binggeli. I had been with him in Lyss in 1978, where I met Lisa. Now, he was in Melbourne to learn English.

Four days later, I continued my journey by bus and hitchhiking and found Peter in White Cliffs after a week. He lived with his wife and two children in an underground house, like all the opal miners in the area. There was even an underground bed and breakfast.

Peter was happy about the visit from Switzerland and the greetings from his sister. He had a metal detector and thanks to it, he had found some small nuggets. I wanted that too. But I didn't have a metal detector yet, and I also wanted to buy a car with my saved money. So, after three weeks, I decided to hitchhike to Brisbane and get a car and a metal detector there.

Peter took me to Wilcannia, where I first had to prove at the police station that I could drive. After five minutes with Peter's old VW bus up and down the street, the outback police officer was satisfied and issued me an Australian driving license. Then I stood on the road in Wilcannia at the Murray River to be taken north to Brisbane, which was 1500 kilometers away. On the first day, I couldn't get away from there and had to sleep under a tree nearby. The next morning, a truck driver took me almost to Brisbane.

In tropical Brisbane, I was able to buy a metal detector and an Australian Ford Falcon caravan cheaply. With this, I drove back to the outback in New South Wales to White Cliffs.

I got to know life in the opal mining fields and started looking for gold with a metal detector, just as Peter had taught me. I found 36 small gold nuggets, which I sold to buy more gasoline for my Ford Falcon."

Phil interrupts: "So that was your plan: to search for gold and gemstones and get rich?"

"Of course, I had naive ideas about searching for gold and gemstones. The idea of discovering a gold vein and getting rich quickly turned out to be an illusion. But the trip to Australia became an adventure that broadened my horizons and is a valuable experience I wouldn't want to miss.

I stayed in the outback for another three months, always hoping to find a larger amount of precious metals. I expanded the search, always leading the metal detector with my left hand, which gave off a monotonous buzzing sound. This noise in my headphones was sometimes interrupted by a tone at a different frequency when I hit something special. The sound was like a cheer and made me dig for bluish-green or golden lumps in the red sand. The sweat poured down my face and didn't dry, becoming more and more, while I nudged stones and got bloody wounds on my calves from the spinifex bushes. Hours and days passed, the big success didn't come. That didn't stop me from continuing, the search alone was inspiring."

"At that time, there were no cell phones or internet. Did you still have contact with Switzerland, especially with Lisa?"

"Once a week, I drove to White Cliffs to buy supplies and always stopped by the post office where I had reserved a box. I sent Lisa a letter every week, and occasionally there was a letter from her in my mailbox.

After three months, she announced that she would come to Australia for a few weeks. I was very happy about her visit.

Before Lisa came to visit me, I wanted to travel once more to the border of Queensland, where some undiscovered gold fields were suspected.

The car and everything needed for the tour of Australia with Lisa was ready. But I wanted to use the month until Lisa's arrival to take my last chance as a gold prospector. I had discussed everything with Peter in the opal village in White Cliffs and then set off towards the border of New South Wales and Queensland.

I only had the things with me that were needed for survival, gold prospecting, and sleeping. Of course, a lot of water and a fly net. Without this fly net over my head, it was impossible to search for gold in this area with concentration and focus. The flies were constantly in the nose, ears, eyes, and wanted to suck up a bit of moisture or sweat from somewhere on the body.

Towards evening, after many kilometers on sand tracks and dirt roads, as the Australians call them, I arrived at a dried-up riverbed and a few eucalyptus trees. According to the old gold prospecting maps, a large historical gold field began here. I could already see from a distance the small hills of sand and gravel that the gold diggers had made four hundred years ago when they used primitive wood/dry air devices to separate the dust, stones, and rubble from the gold. They called them dry blowers because water was needed for survival back then and not for washing gold.

I had lit a small fire next to the eucalyptus tree and my Ford Falcon, cooked a soup, and grilled a sausage. While eating, I could watch some kangaroos staring at me with interest and then hopping away. As dusk fell, the birds sang their evening song, and the laughing kookaburra laughed almost like a human. They belong to the kingfisher family and live only in Australia, Tasmania, and New Guinea. They grow almost 50 centimeters long, are brown-gray, and have a white chest. Kookaburra means 'trickster' and 'laughing Hans'.

When it got dark, I lay down on the mattress in the back of the Ford. With a flashlight, I studied the old maps again.

Early in the morning, after a tea and a piece of hard bread, I went with the metal detector to the first hill to get an overview of the landscape. The sun had just risen, and I could see into the distance. I saw hundreds of identical hills and small valleys, but also places where the old gold diggers had dug. I knew that in such an area, a systematic approach would bring the most success. So, I first wandered for half an hour in a dried-up creek bed. In such creeks, gold was washed down after a heavy rain, and when everything dried up, the nugget smiled at you directly, you just had to pick it up. Unfortunately, this ideal case happens very rarely. I had made such a lucky find only once.

After an hour, I left the area and climbed more hills, systematically searching other creeks and the areas where the old gold diggers had left their traces. It was already early afternoon when I took a break and had my lunch with water. I climbed another hill and then slowly walked back to the bush camp where my car was parked. After an unsuccessful search at this location as well, I began the return journey. Feeling my way back in the direction I had come from.

After an hour, I still didn't see the car, and everything looked the same. Slowly, I started to worry. Stories came to my mind that I had read in a book about the indigenous people of Australia. The Aborigines used to always travel on foot, walking hundreds of kilometers across the continent and never getting lost. They called their paths 'dream paths' and 'song lines'. For insiders, song lines are invisible labyrinthine paths that traverse the entire Australian continent. A song was like a map and a kind of compass. If you knew the song, you could always find your way through the land. The ancestors scattered notes and footprints on their travels, so-called dream paths, a kind of traffic route between far-flung tribes of the natives.

On another hill, which was slightly higher than all the others, I took a break. I wondered if I was really lost. In which direction was my car and the campsite? I regretted not knowing a song line and realized that I was not on a dream path. I let my gaze wander over the endless expanse with the countless hills and sank into a meditative state. In five hours, the sun would set, and I would have to spend the night in the wilderness if I didn't make it back to the starting point in time. I figured that I would survive it, but there was only a little water left in my bottle.

Since I had been dealing with religions and questions of meaning for a few years and had also read many books about the wisdom of life, the term 'pilgrimage' came to mind. In early Christianity, there were two types of pilgrimages, I remembered. To walk for God (ambulare pro Deo), following the example of Christ, or Father Abraham, who left the city of Ur in Babylon and lived in a tent from then on.

The other type of pilgrimage was a pilgrimage as punishment. Those who had committed a serious crime (peccata enormia) were required, based on fixed tariffs, to take on the role of the wandering beggar. This meant begging on the road with a hat, wallet, staff, and badge, seeking salvation. This idea that 'walking' or 'wandering' would atone for a committed crime goes back to the wanderings imposed on Cain in the Bible to atone for the murder of his brother Abel.

On my pilgrimage, neither applied, I thought. But being in the desert also meant, in ancient times, finding the way to God or oneself there!

And me? I want to find my way back to the car and not spend the night out here or die of thirst, I told myself. My inner voice advised me to keep walking. I did so. I took a sip of water from the almost empty bottle and walked. I hummed a song and thought about the song lines of the natives. The song lines were their compass and showed them the way. There was hardly a rock, a creek, a hill, or even animals that could not be sung about or had already been sung about. One had to imagine the song lines as spaghetti that wriggled here and there, with each episode being read from the geological formations. By episode, the natives understood "sacred site."

By singing the world into existence, the ancestors were poets — in the original meaning of the word "poesis", which meant creation. No "Abo" could imagine that the created world would be in any way imperfect. His religious life had only the goal of preserving the land as it was and as it should be. This explains why the railway and road builders as well as the mining companies are constantly in conflict with the natives of the land.

Another pilgrimage is the one to Santiago de Compostela in the far west of northern Spain, to a place of pilgrimage with an archbishop's seat. The tomb of Saint James is said to be there. The Camino de Santiago ends there, and many people walk hundreds of kilometers through half of Europe in search of God, themselves, or simply the meaning of life.

With these thoughts, I had already been wandering for an hour, looking for a dirt road, a path, or a eucalyptus tree under which my Ford Falcon could be. It felt like searching for a sacred site, as in the episode of the natives.

Again, I took my water bottle, it was 37 degrees warm and dry, and I was terribly thirsty. I put the bottle to my mouth, and with three gulps, the bottle was empty. I furrowed my sweaty brow and was at the end of my adventurous spirit. I had actually gotten lost and didn't know what to do next. In which direction should I go now?

I had a vivid imagination and started to imagine myself — like in a mirage — sitting relaxed by the sea in a deck chair with a cold drink in my hand. But after five minutes, I wandered on and hummed my favorite song by John Lennon: Imagine!

The sun was setting, and I estimated that it would be light for at best another hour until sunset. I wandered on, always looking into the distance, but also back, from where I had come. Courage and optimism, which had always accompanied me, seemed to be leaving me. My eyes searched into the distance when I suddenly saw a small dot moving on a hill on the horizon. I walked faster towards this point but couldn't make out what it was.

With my last strength, I started to run and stumble. A binocular would have been useful now. I believed to see that the point was moving. I ran even faster, breathing heavily in that direction.

Now I was close enough to this hill and saw that there was definitely a person. I started shouting, but the person didn't react. I thought it could be a gold prospector with a detector and headphones who couldn't hear me. I approached this person on the small hill, shouted, waved, and jumped into the air when the man suddenly turned around, took off the headphones, and looked in my direction. He waved and gave me a sign that he had noticed me.

When I finally reached the prospector, we greeted each other. I immediately noticed that the man couldn't be Australian. We started talking. Where are you from, have you found gold? The man's name was Yuri, he came from Russia, and so far, he hadn't found any nuggets in the old gold fields here either. But he knew where his jeep was. I confessed to him that I couldn't find my car anymore and only had one goal: to find a living being that could help me. Yuri said that he knew this situation and therefore never went out of sight of his jeep in this area up here. I became thoughtful but also grateful that I had some kind of compass or a song line that had guided me to the saving Yuri.

Yuri said that he wanted to break off his search anyway, go back to his jeep, and then continue on the bumpy road to the lodge just before the border with Queensland. He showed me his jeep in the distance, down in a small valley, which he never lost sight of while searching for gold. If he continued searching behind another hill, he would always return to the jeep and drive to a place where he could see the vehicle.

That was a lesson for me on how not to lose orientation in the bush and not get lost, but also a sign of how in life sometimes a detour can lead to the goal.

Yuri said that he would take me with him. There was only one bumpy road, and it would certainly lead us to my car. And that's how it was. I was saved and grateful for this fate. In the past hours, I had experienced the feeling of being lost in the wilderness without water and orientation and realizing that the situation was life-threatening. I could have died alone in the middle of nowhere."

*

Phil is visibly impressed by Beat's adventurous story. "I assume that you soon changed your emigration plans afterward."

"Yes, after just three months in the outback, I realized that it would be a mistake to want to stay in Australia. However, the adventure in Australia turned out to be one of the most valuable experiences of my life."

"I can understand that. It broadened your horizons and was certainly beneficial for your professional career later on. By the way, I noticed that you have good knowledge of the Bible and that you seem to be interested in religions", remarks Phil. "Do you want to talk about it, or is that too personal for you?"

Phil's question surprises Beat, but he responds spontaneously and openly: "Yes, of course, we can talk about it. As I said, I have been interested in religions since I was young, as I told you about the pilgrimages of early Christianity that I remembered. The search for meaning in life and the question of the right faith have indeed always occupied me and are still exciting topics that I like to discuss today.

They are also part of my book that I am writing, and I would like to discuss them with you."

"That makes me happy, also that you express your views openly because every person can and should determine for themselves what they believe in."

"I have already read many books on the topics of faith, church, and religion and have written down my thoughts on them. I am curious to hear what you think about it."

# On the Search for Meaning

The search for the "right" faith was a long process for Beat, a path with many turns, some of which proved to be right and others that did not align with his beliefs. In his oldest diaries, Beat finds many entries from the time when he was already interested in questions of faith and religion as a teenager and young adult.

## The Conversion

As a student, Beat attended Sunday school and religious instruction in the Evangelical Reformed Church in Biel and was confirmed, just like most of his peers he knew. Beyond that, churches and religion were not topics that interested him passionately as a fifteen-year-old. He was all the more surprised when one day an acquaintance of his parents asked if he could give him the book "Jesus Our Destiny" by Wilhelm Busch as a gift.

Beat hesitated briefly before accepting it with thanks. He only knew Wilhelm Busch as the poet and illustrator of "Max and Moritz", but he quickly realized that the author of the book he was holding was a German theologian of the same name.

After reading the book, Beat, as the author recommended, decided for Jesus. According to Wilhelm Busch, Jesus was the only savior and the only one who could take away the burden of guilt from poor sinners. Beat had converted and subsequently attended the popular tent evangelizations at the time. Initially, nothing happened until he got into a conversation with Robert Nydegger, a leading member of the local free church. It was about questions of life and what our existence in this world means.

Although Beat was now convinced that he had found his direction of faith, as Robert correctly noted, he was unfortunately not a regular churchgoer. Therefore, Robert invited the newly converted Beat to visit the Free Mission Church in Bern with him.

The Free Mission Church had an inviting and relaxed way of conveying its message. Beat particularly liked the family gatherings. At that time, it was known that free churches conducted so-called evangelizations. What was preached there was exactly what was written in Wilhelm Busch's book. At the end of the sermon, visitors who were not yet converted and born again were invited to stand up and come forward. There, they prayed, and if the addressed individuals requested it with a YES, their sins were forgiven, and they could start a new life. Whenever possible, of course, in the corresponding free church.

Beat subsequently occasionally visited the Free Mission Church but also went a few times to the Evangelical Baptist Church in Diessbach. This was where Manfred Baumgartner was a member and part of the church leadership. Now Beat understood why Manfred had earlier drawn his attention to Wilhelm Busch's teachings. Every newborn Christian has the task of spreading the message so that the addressed person can realize that without conversion, they are a sinner, and only Jesus can forgive these sins. Without conversion, the sinner would be lost.

At this time, Beat considered studying theology at the university. He was invited to an interview in Bern, and Professor Marti explained the long path he would have to take to complete a theology degree. During the conversation, Beat felt that this could not really be his path, and he told the professor that he had ultimately decided differently: he wanted to study business administration, travel the world, and earn money.

*"My inner compass kept me from choosing a path in life that I was not meant for."*

From 1976 to 1982, other questions took precedence for Beat over religious ones. The most important goals were completing his apprenticeship as a metal construction technician and then further professional training. In between, Beat fulfilled another great wish: he began to discover the world. Together with Lisa, he traveled to Israel, where they worked in a kibbutz for four months.

His second major trip lasted longer. With a one-way ticket for emigrants in his pocket, he traveled to Australia.

Before returning to Switzerland, Lisa had visited him Down Under, but after a year in Australia, Beat buried his emigration plans. Together they returned to Switzerland and started to plan their lives anew: getting married, working, having children, and building a house.

At first, they lived with Lisa's parents in Hardern, and Beat decided to first complete the distance learning course with Saturday classes in business administration. He achieved this after three years, and before completing it, he got a job as a calculator and project manager at Metall-bau Diethelm in Burgdorf in 1985.

Beat and Lisa got married. The wedding took place on June 16, 1984, in the old church in Lyss. After that, the couple moved to Burgdorf, where their daughters Claudia and Conny were born in 1986 and 1987.

Now everything seemed to be on track — but was that the fulfillment of all dreams?

The questions of meaning that Robert Nydegger had asked him years earlier had never completely left Beat's mind.

*Where do we go after death?*

Beat searched for answers and read books by Elisabeth Kübler-Ross, the well-known near-death researcher and end-of-life counselor at the time. Could it be that after physical death, the spirit or soul of the deceased continues to live in a world invisible to us? He found no convincing answer. Only hints, speculations, and vaguely justified claims suggested that no one knows if and how we will continue to live in an afterlife. Beat could not have known then that forty years later, he would have his own near-death experience.

"So, I leave these questions unanswered and content myself with that", Beat wrote in his diary.


## Honeymoon Trip to India

After their wedding, Beat and Lisa traveled to India in 1984. It was one of their first forays into distant lands, followed by many other major journeys in later years.

They flew with Air India to Mumbai, the bustling metropolis of the state of Maharashtra, which fascinated them with its diversity and energy. The architecture of the Victorian buildings and the extreme contrasts between great poverty and wealth impressed them equally.

Beat had previously informed himself a little about the societal structure of the Indian population and knew that this country with its 1.4 billion inhabitants prides itself on its religious freedom. The largest religious group is the Hindus, followed by Muslims, Christians, Sikhs, and Buddhists. People are assigned to a caste (Varna) at birth, to which they belong for life. Beat had learned that religious freedom here meant that the religious communities live peacefully side by side. However, it should not be interpreted as everyone being able to choose freely between different religions.

The four main castes are each assigned a color: white for the highly respected Brahmins (mostly merchants), red for Kshatriyas (originally warriors), yellow for Vaishyas (farmers, merchants), and black for Shudras (servants and day laborers). Outside of these castes are the Untouchables, also called Pariahs. Increasingly, the "Untouchables" feel their status is discriminatory and consider themselves descendants of the indigenous people of India.

Beat was sure that even the poorest people in India, that is, hundreds of millions of people, have their dreams.

*But do they have a real chance to fulfill their dreams?*


## Journey to Goa

After a few days in Mumbai, they traveled by Indian Railways to Goa, a small coastal town with an exciting history. Goa had been occupied and influenced by the Portuguese during the colonial era, leading to a unique blend of Indian and European culture. Beat and Lisa learned that Goa had become a popular destination for dropouts in the 1960s, seeking freedom, spirituality, and an alternative lifestyle. The beaches, the relaxed atmosphere, and the low cost of living attracted many young travelers.

In Goa, Beat met a Swiss dropout named Markus, who was on a quest to escape the "Swiss narrow-mindedness and pedantry." Markus participated in the legendary parties each evening, where drugs were also involved, and hoped to find happiness there.

Beat started a conversation with Markus about the meaning of life and asked him about his life goal. Markus took some time to think before answering, "My life goal? It's simple, I want to live authentically. To be myself, you know, free from societal expectations and conventions. You won't find happiness here in material things, but in a feeling of inner contentment."

Beat recognized parallels between Markus's search for self-discovery and authenticity and his own travel experiences. He shared with Markus the belief that true happiness and the meaning of life are not found in external factors or conventions, but in the individual discovery and development of one's personality and life goals.


## Journey to Kerala

From Goa, Beat and Lisa embarked on an adventurous journey by bus to Kerala, a state in southwestern India. They traveled overland and experienced firsthand the challenges and beauties of Indian transportation. They rode in crowded trains, night buses, and old taxis with creaking gearboxes. The journey was sometimes arduous, but they came to appreciate the hospitality of the people.

In Kerala, they spent two days on a houseboat that took them through the famous backwaters. The backwaters are a network of lagoons, lakes, and rivers characterized by lush nature and tranquil beauty. During the trip, they could enjoy the idyllic landscape, observe passing villages, and absorb the serenity of the surroundings.

Beat found not only outer beauty but also inner peace and tranquility in such places. He practiced mindfulness by living consciously in the moment, opening his senses, and focusing on his surroundings. He watched the ocean waves, listened to the rustling of the palm forests, and felt the gentle wind on his skin. In this conscious perception, he was able to establish a deeper connection with himself and the world around him. It was a place where he could let his thoughts come to rest and find inner balance.

In Kerala, the Christian part of southern India, Beat struck up a conversation on the houseboat with a fellow traveler, an older gentleman named Gupta. Gupta was the name of an ancient Indian dynasty, but the older man said he belonged to the Christian religion. Beat took the opportunity to hear from Gupta how Christianity came to India.

Gupta explained that many Christians live in Kerala because this part of India came into contact with Christianity early on. It is believed that Christianity was brought to India by the Apostle Thomas in the first century. Thomas preached the gospel and founded communities along the Malabar coast.

Beat asked Gupta about the difference between Christianity and the Hindu religion.

"In Hinduism, there are a multitude of gods and goddesses, while Christianity believes in one God, with the Trinity of Father, Son, and Holy Spirit", said Gupta, continuing in the style of a scholar. "The concept of the end of life is also different. In Hinduism, there is the concept of reincarnation, with the aim of breaking out of the cycle of rebirths and attaining salvation, while Christians believe in eternal life after death, which depends on their actions and faith in Jesus Christ."

Although Beat did not have a concept of eternal life after death, he and Gupta finally agreed that despite these differences, the fundamental goal for both religions was to do good and believe in a higher power that helps us navigate life successfully.

"How do we receive the messages of this higher power, and how do we know which path we should take?" asked Beat.

"We humans all have a universal navigation system", Gupta answered with conviction. "Regardless of our culture and religion. When you are lost, you must listen to your inner voice."

Beat nodded, "So, to my inner compass..."

"That's nicely said", praised Gupta, looking out from the boat at the vast backwater with its palm forests and rice fields. "When your compass is on, it's like a GPS: You always know where you are."

## Church Communities

Ecclesiastically, Beat and Lisa were engaged with the Free Mission Community (FMG) in Oberburg/Burgdorf. One becomes a member of a mission community by unconditionally accepting the Holy Scripture as the basis of faith, believing in Jesus Christ as a personal Lord, and actively participating in community life. Adult baptism as a confession of faith is taught and practiced.

Beat wanted to understand the reasons and significance of adult baptism from the pastor. "What would happen if I didn't get baptized as an adult? I was already baptized as a child!"

"Dear Beat", the pastor began warmly. "I can tell you that baptism is a very important and symbolic act in the Christian tradition. It symbolizes entry into the community of believers and the beginning of a new life in faith in Jesus Christ. If you decide not to get baptized, there are no direct consequences. Everyone has the right to make their own decisions regarding baptism. However, it is important to know that baptism is a way to publicly declare that you have found your faith in Jesus Christ and are part of the community of believers."

Who is that important for, Beat wondered. He felt a need to belong to a community of faith, but to be baptized again? "Isn't it enough that I have converted?"

"As a converted Christian, you can certainly continue to be active in the church and live out your faith", said the pastor patiently. "But a baptism can also be an important way to publicly affirm your decision to live your life with Jesus Christ and to reaffirm your commitment to the faith. It is important that you weigh your decision carefully, and it is good that you talk to others about it. You can also discuss it with a spiritual mentor to ensure that you feel comfortable and understand what baptism symbolizes."

Beat found this too vague. He wanted more concrete answers and asked, "Will I be saved then, go to paradise, and have eternal life, as the Bible says?"

"Let me elaborate briefly. In many Christian churches, baptism is seen as a sacrament that symbolizes the cleansing of sin and incorporation into the Christian community. However, baptism alone does not guarantee eternal life in paradise. Christians believe that salvation is achieved through God's grace and the acceptance of Jesus Christ as Lord and Savior. Baptism is not the only criterion for salvation and eternal life in paradise."

"Yes, okay, I understand that. But what's the benefit to me?"

The pastor's patience seemed unwavering. He calmly continued: "It is important to understand that salvation is a gift from God, based on faith and trust in Jesus Christ. Baptism is an expression of this faith and the desire to follow Jesus. Therefore, it is important not only to be baptized but also to accept faith in Jesus Christ and align your life accordingly. This means living according to God's will, striving to serve others, and growing in love."

Beat had no more questions: "Alright, so let's get on with it and get baptized in Lake Biel!"

Beat and Lisa were persuaded to be baptized as adults, as Jesus was once by John the Baptist. The ceremony took place at Lake Biel near the country inn of Rütte-Gut between Ipsach and Sutz. It was a joyful experience. Beat and Lisa had already been baptized as children, but free churches say that a child cannot decide whether to accept this faith with the forgiveness of sins.

## Goddard's Law of Attraction

The free church customs and rituals had something spiritual and esoteric for Beat, which he was open to, but his search for the meaning of life was not ended, as another big question increasingly occupied him: Where am I going?

*Where do I come from, where am I, where do I want to go?*

Beat read about Neville Goddard's *Law of Assumption* and was fascinated. He wanted to develop spiritually and live according to the *Law of Freedom*, as Goddard sometimes called it himself, or according to the *Law of Attraction*, as later authors like Michael J. Losier, Victoria Lakefield, and many others formulated it.

What particularly impressed Beat was a kind of guide to manifesting, that is, having a vision and imagining that one has already achieved what one wants to achieve. One must believe in oneself and be convinced that one will reach the manifested goal if one meditates for a few minutes daily and imagines how it would feel to know that one has already achieved what one has set as a goal.

That sounds so simple and cannot, of course, be that simple, thought Beat, but his curiosity was piqued, and he decided to delve deeper into the Law of Attraction.

Neville Goddard died on October 1, 1972, in Los Angeles, and his books have found millions of readers worldwide.

### Neville Goddard

In his work, he deals with the human imagination and what it can achieve. He uses the Bible as an example and explains, using biblical stories, what they mean in a figurative sense. He always said that the stories of the Bible are not to be understood literally but always symbolize a wisdom. In his lectures, he always called on his audience to refute his work and verify for themselves whether what he reported could be true. He did not demand blind obedience and faith from his students but urged them to disprove his claims. Only through applying it themselves would they recognize the truth.

For Beat, Goddard's theories were a revelation, especially in relation to his own previous experiences in dealing with faith, religion, and the — depending on the church — different views on how to earn God's grace. According to Goddard, there is only one master, despite all the gods in some religions, and this master is God in me, in my SELF.

This sentence opened doors for Beat that he had not seen before. The kingdom of heaven and paradise do not wait for us somewhere; everything is within us, waiting to be discovered.

God is not to be found somewhere, neither above the clouds nor as an invisible figure on earth, to determine every individual fate.

Religious missionaries bind people to themselves and their faith community; they interpret and determine the rules of behavior and rituals on how to ask for forgiveness to be freed from the burden of sin.

Beat was no longer a convinced member of the free churches and left the mission community after a long internal struggle. He did this with mixed feelings, knowing that religious institutions, regardless of their faith direction, offer many people what they seek: support and comfort.

## New Tasks

By the late 1980s, Beat's life was marked by professional and residential changes. He worked as a sales manager and later as a strategic planning manager at Ascom before taking a position as Product & Service Manager at the PTT General Directorate in Bern in 1990.

He and Lisa found a house in Bargen, where they moved in with their children. Bargen, near Aarberg, was the ideal place for him. With three children by this time — son Flavio had also been born — Beat did not want to live in a city but in the countryside, yet still close to essential infrastructures.

Soon after settling in, Beat was approached by the Evangelical Reformed Church, asking if he would directly run for president. After some contemplation on his spiritual path, Beat accepted the role and served joyfully and with new ideas for ten years alongside Pastor Johnson Eliezer. As president, Beat placed great importance on regional cooperation with the surrounding communities of Aarberg, Kallnach, Kappelen, and Lyss. Johnson was wholeheartedly involved with his enthusiasm and brilliant messages, contributing as a singer and guitarist.

Johnson, now retired, became active again in September 2023, supporting the Kallnach church part-time. Beat occasionally visits him there.

## Trust in: YOURSELF

Beat's inner compass led him to success. His journey from school, apprenticeship, travels, further education, career, leisure, and family was unconsciously and consciously shaped by his optimistic mindset.

Some doors opened as if by themselves, not merely by chance, but because Beat manifested his desires, and they fulfilled themselves according to the law of attraction. Throughout his career from 1990 until his retirement in 2022, he no longer had to send out job applications. Positions as Sales Director at Unisource, later as Head of Key Account Management, and finally as Director of Sales & Marketing for Swisscom's largest customers were offered to him.

Beat's compass told him he was on the right path. Over the years, he developed his own method to harmonize with himself and the world. He realized that creation, the entire cosmos, and all earthly things are part of God. He concluded that God is within each of us, a teaching also held by pantheists. He was delighted and strengthened in his faith when he found in literature that even the non-denominational Albert Einstein leaned towards pantheistic thinking.

**The Gratitude and Success Journal**

"You asked about my religious views, and you see, I did not find it easy to answer that question", says Beat. They sit in the cafeteria they have chosen for their regular meetings, and he watches Phil remove his reading glasses and turn to him.

"No, you didn't make it easy for yourself", confirms the neurologist. "You went a long way, converting through free church rituals and getting baptized as an adult, but later left the free church after reading Goddard's theories and ultimately found God within yourself. Am I interpreting this correctly?"

"Summarized briefly, that's right. Since then, I live in a feeling of harmony, and for that, I am grateful. By the way, after leaving the free church, I remained a member of another church community, the Evangelical Reformed Church in my region, and even served as its president for a time. I still occasionally attend the Sunday sermons in Kallnach and Bargen. For me, this is not contradictory, even though I have a different concept of faith than most churchgoers."

"And there are fewer and fewer of them", Phil notes thoughtfully. "About a third of the Swiss population is now registered as non-denominational, and the national churches are suffering from a massive loss of members. How do you feel about this development?"

Beat is aware of this trend and has explanations for it: "For a long time, churches dictated how people should live, but now they are becoming obsolete. They have lost much trust and are no longer the cornerstones of our system. There are many reasons for this, and even religious people are leaving the church."

"You found a veritable substitute for religion in Goddard's theories. Do you also pray? Forgive me, this is again indiscreet, but I'm curious because you don't assume God is somewhere in heaven but feel Him within yourself. So, whom would you turn to if you wanted to pray?"

It's a good question, Beat thinks. But it doesn't throw him off; he is even glad for Phil's genuine interest in him and his faith. "It's only logical that you would ask such a question, for it would be contradictory in my case to ask an invisible God in heaven for help and support. 'Help yourself, and God will help you' is a trite saying, but it has a true core.

*God is not only in me but in each of us.*

We all have our soul, our compass, our conscience, and our awareness of what feels right and good and what is evil or harmful. I do not pray but receive divine energy within me in meditative moments, and for that, I am grateful."

Beat has not had such an intense discussion for quite a while. Phil is visibly pleased and follows up on Beat's statement: "Grateful? Whom do you thank then?"

"I write in my gratitude and success journal daily if possible. It helped me, for example, to prepare myself with positive thoughts for my last surgery, where I had bypasses installed in my heart. I have been practicing this ritual for several years, not just since I've been in this clinic. I often combine it with meditation and take the necessary time for it."

## Fitness and Sports

Phil and Beat sit opposite each other on the 15th floor of the Inselspital café, enjoying a magnificent view of the city and the wide expanse of the Gurten and the Alps. The scene somewhat reminds Beat of the book by Strelecky: *"The Café on the Edge of the World."*

"I must say, I am impressed by the path you have taken", notes the scientist. "Family, career, major travels, further education, and alongside all that, you always had time for sports activities. How did you manage to balance it all?"

### Swimming, Cycling, and Marathon Running

"You're right", laughs Beat. "Sports have always been important to me, as a balance to school life, later during my apprenticeship and career. Sports strengthened my body and generated mental strength in me. I competed in bike races and was good at it. That was also good for my self-confidence and self-esteem. At sporting events, I felt liberated. There was no room for thoughts about questions like where I come from, why I'm here, and where I'm going."

"So, being able to occasionally put those questions aside was important to you?"

"These questions are important and must be asked, but you shouldn't constantly let them run through your mind like a mantra."

"I understand", nods Phil. "Did you have specific athletic goals? Did you want to become famous as an athlete?"

"No, no medals or elite sports. Family and career always came first for me. But it was fun to swim long distances, participate in bike races and marathons, compete in the Murten–Fribourg run, the Lake Brienz and Greifensee runs, and to reach the finish line of the hundred-kilometer Biel run."

"So, unlike me, you're quite an athlete", Phil says appreciatively.

"Well", says Beat modestly. "Being fit gives you a good feeling; it helps you face challenges. When I was around thirty, I discovered my fascination for motorcycle racing. Motorcycling was a new challenge for me."

"How? You participated in motorcycle races?" asks Phil, astonished.

"Yes, that was an exciting time. On November 5, 2021, the *Bieler Tagblatt* featured a photo of World Champion Dominique Aegerter and me on the front page, and in the sports section, they extensively reported on us under the headline 'Gasoline in the Blood.' By the way, I've written down everything about how I got to experience Moto GP races live", says Beat, grinning.

## Motorcycle Racing

Beat already had a license for 125 cc motorcycles. Switching to powerful bikes was thus a mere formality. He was in his mid-thirties when he bought a used touring Yamaha with a 1200 cc engine and took the test with it. After that, he could get the endorsement for the big machines stamped.

Lisa was not pleased that he often rode early on Saturday mornings via Chasseral in the Jura and along the Doubs. Soon, the French Jura also became his target area for day trips. In Goumois, Saint-Ursanne, or La Chaux-de-Fonds, he crossed the border into France. Beat greatly enjoyed curving on the French asphalt. Somehow, the surface was grippier and slightly orange-colored. Importantly, there was little traffic in the remote Jura region at that time. In a traditional restaurant popular among motorcyclists in the small French village of Saint-Hippolyte, he always met other motorcycle enthusiasts who enjoyed café et croissants in the garden and praised the curve experiences and the wonderful topography of the Jura. The license plates of the parked motorcycles — BE, AG, JU, BS, SO, NE, and even ZH — indicated that many Swiss people took breaks here.

Soon, Beat found the second-hand machine too cumbersome. It was too sluggish in the curves and acceleration. So, he traded his bike at Moto Sport Möri for an agile Yamaha Fazer with slightly less horsepower and displacement. Occasionally, he took his eldest daughter Claudia along on the pillion seat.

More and more, the fascination of riding had gripped him. Flying and gravitational forces, the complete immersion in the riding dynamics with the invisible energies, combined with a high and desireless well-being in the here and now, thrilled him.

Wanting to learn new things, he signed up for a two-day training session at the Anneau du Rhin racetrack in Alsace. Upon arrival, the participants were first theoretically prepared for the track. Anticipatory driving was the order of the day. This didn't mean staring ahead but "reading the road." After the theory, it was onto the track to test centrifugal and gyroscopic forces and lean angles on two wheels. Some crashed because they were going too fast. Beat was more cautious and let faster riders who wanted to push their limits pass.

The course had sparked in Beat the desire for a faster motorcycle better suited to a racetrack than his touring bike. In the mid-90s, motorcycles with as many horsepower as kilograms were trending. Yamaha made this its advertising slogan for the new R1: 180 HP and 180 kg light. This was the bike ridden by Valentino Rossi in the GP circus. He won almost every race with the R1.

Interested, Beat followed the Moto GP race events, on TV and directly at international racetracks in Italy, Portugal, France, and Germany. At that time, Swisscom founded the internet company Blue Window, and the advertising carrier Tom Lüthi was sponsored by Blue Window. A research engineer Beat knew was responsible for technology in Tom Lüthi's team at the time. This gave Beat access to so-called paddock tickets, allowing him to experience the action in Tom Lüthi's box and on the racetrack live.

He then bought an R1 at his Moto Center in Aarberg, influenced by Yamaha's advertising slogan. On this bike, Beat rode more lying down than sitting. This feeling of oneness with a means of transportation had already interested King Charles V in riding art with a horse, sometimes more than state affairs. Charles wondered whether the horse was a part of the rider or the rider a part of the horse.

Beat signed up for a training session on the racetrack in Dijon. Yamaha Switzerland organized this event, renting the track for two days with a team of mechanics and trainers. The bikes had to be slightly adjusted for this training. Turn signals were removed, and tires changed. This was done in the pits at the racetrack before the training. Slicks were mounted, tires without tread and grooves.

After checking into the hotel, Beat strolled through Dijon's old town, past Romanesque-Gothic cathedrals, and found a restaurant where several Swiss people were already enjoying an aperitif. They were also participating in the training on the racetrack the next day. The conversations mostly revolved around motorcycling and riding dynamics with lean angles, but Dijon's palaces, churches, and towers were also a topic. Especially the owl in the protected zone on Place Darcy attracted the interest of the Swiss motorcycle fans. According to legend, this owl fulfills the wishes of the person who strokes it with their left hand.

### *The fascination with magical forces...*

After dinner, everyone went to their hotels early. They all wanted to be rested and clear-headed the next morning. The goal of the training was to learn the limits of riding without taking life-threatening risks.

Well-rested, Beat rode his R1 to the racetrack about fifteen kilometers outside Dijon right after breakfast. The Dijon-Prenois racetrack is demanding and very hilly. In professional circles, it is called the little green hell. Notable sections are the roughly 1.2-kilometer-long start/finish straight and the Parabolique, a tight right-hand curve with a steep incline. The track length is 3.8 kilometers. Dijon-Prenois is a natural track like the Nürburgring and is one of the most interesting racetracks near Switzerland. After an hour of theory about the track, riding technique, and materials, Beat took a slow inspection ride with a small group.

By noon, everyone was ready to ride on their own following the trainers' instructions. Beat enjoyed the curves, especially the 1.2-kilometer-long straight. There, he could push his R1 to the top speed of 230 km/h without limits. Beat had great respect for this speed directly in the wind and in nature. He couldn't achieve a flow state at that speed. It required incredible concentration. It was strenuous and not really enjoyable. Beat preferred the curves with lean angles taken at 80 to 100 km/h. He then usually rode the long straight at only 150 to 160 km/h because he didn't need to win a race.

In the afternoon, there was another theory session before the final laps. Like in the morning, Beat rode at his own pace on the straight, others overtaking him. It didn't matter to him. It was not a race, although lap times were measured. The track record was set by Formula 1 driver Alain Prost in 2015. He drove at an average speed of 215 km/h.

Beat leaned his R1 in the final curve at about 80 km/h and rode towards the finish line at about 170 km/h when suddenly a rider behind him crashed into his bike. It is a habit of racers and unfortunately also amateurs to close up as close as possible to the rear wheel of the rider in front. Beat and the rider behind him crashed on the straight. Emergency services quickly arrived, treated them, and took them to the hospital in Dijon. Beat was diagnosed with broken ribs and, of course, bruises. Two days later, he was transferred to Aarberg Hospital, where he recovered for a week. The R1 was totaled, and Beat's motorcycle days were over for the time being.


## Boat Rides

On Beat's occasional trips to the nearby Lake Biel, he always remembers a particular day from his childhood and sees himself with his father on a small fishing boat moored in the Zihl Canal.

On an early morning in the summer of 1967, they took the boat out to the mouth of the Aare Canal, where several other fishing boats were already waiting. They waited for the fish to bite, especially the perch, which was highly sought after and the most commonly caught fish in Swiss lakes. The sun rose at six o'clock that June morning, but it was already warm, and a hot day was expected, so Beat's father wanted to return to the harbor by noon. Beat, only eight years old, was allowed to fish with a small rod.

Soon, the perch began to bite, and after forty minutes, they had already caught a dozen. The first pleasure boats sped past them, accelerating quickly with their powerful engines. Beat marveled at how the beautiful boats slowly entered the planing phase and roared toward Petersinsel. He asked his father why he didn't buy such a boat. "Then we could go water skiing after fishing, or you could tow me on an inflatable boat!"

His father looked at him with little understanding. "What kind of ideas do you have? Aren't you satisfied with my boat? These pleasure boats cost a lot of money and use thirty liters of gasoline per hour. That's out of the question for me!"

Beat's first dream. He never forgot it.

Beat fell silent and imagined what it would be like to be in such a boat with cushioned seats. He let his imagination run wild and forgot about fishing for a moment. He told himself that when he grew up and earned a lot of money, he would buy such a boat. They returned to the dock with more than twenty fish in the boat. Beat was still dreaming…

Twenty-five years later, Beat passed the boating test on Lake Biel and had the financial means to afford such a boat. He bought a Bayliner from the Herzog-Werft in Alpnach near Lucerne. Three years later, he traded it in for a new Larson, a bowrider. He was proud of this boat, which had enough space for his whole family — Lisa and their three children, Claudia, Conny, and Flavio — and the boat spot in the Barken-hafen in Nidau. A long-held wish had come true. For Beat, it was further proof that dreams can come true.

## The Captain's Responsibility

When the weather was nice on weekends, they planned trips on the lake. With water skis and wakeboards, they would head toward Petersinsel. So it was on a Sunday in July, when the weather forecast predicted hot weather and the possibility of local thunderstorms. Their friends, the couple Jakob and Salome, were with them. Early in the afternoon, a storm approached from the west near the island. Beat knew that the weather on Lake Biel could change quickly, especially when the Joran wind arose, an unpredictable downdraft that sometimes developed into a hurricane-like storm at the southern foot of the Jura.

They decided to glide to the Hotel-Restaurant Rousseau to take a break and let the storm pass. The name of the restaurant always reminded Beat of Jean-Jacques Rousseau, the philosopher and Enlightenment thinker who had lived on the nearby Petersinsel for two months in 1765. From history lessons, Beat remembered Rousseau as one of the pioneers of the French Revolution and an advocate of the "Back to Nature" movement. For Rousseau, the two months on Lake Biel were the happiest time in his life — at least that's what the philosopher wrote years later in his book "Confessions and Reveries."

The lake was still mirror-smooth, but something was brewing from Neuchâtel.

The boat glided effortlessly over the lake at 60 km/h. Beat wondered if the weather would allow them to safely cover the 25 kilometers back to Barkenhafen after the break. With high waves, the return trip could become arduous.

He remembered that, as captain, he bore the responsibility. At the dock in front of Hotel Rousseau, he secured the boat. They went to the sun terrace, ordered drinks, and ice cream for everyone. Jakob, not often on the lake, asked Beat how he assessed the situation. "In the worst case, we could stay at the hotel overnight and return tomorrow. That wouldn't be a problem", Jakob said with a grin.

Beat was still undecided: "We'll watch the weather and decide then. You just need to know that we will only make slow progress if the water is turbulent, and it will take much longer to reach the harbor. It could take more than an hour and be a wild ride. If there are dense clouds and poor visibility, I would need a compass. But this boat doesn't have one."

In the 1990s, there were no smartphones, without which hardly any-one leaves the house today. Navigation and compass apps were unimag-inable at that time.

Beat became thoughtful and seemed unsure of how to decide. But Jakob and Salome reassured him, saying they trusted him and were con-fident he would make the right decision.

After half an hour, they saw that the weather on the lake had indeed calmed down. The orange flashing lights on the shore were still sending warning signals, but they would likely be turned off soon as the storm had subsided. Beat checked the boat again before deciding to return. They boarded, and Beat started the engine. He gave it little gas while carefully steering the boat through the calm waters. Suddenly, a strong wind picked up again, and the bowrider began to sway. Beat struggled to keep it under control. The waves grew higher, and the boat rocked. Everyone tried to hold on to the sides of the boat as Beat desperately tried to keep it on course.

The situation became even more threatening when a lightning bolt struck nearby. A huge wave, unlike any Beat had ever seen on the usually calm lake, hit the boat and nearly capsized it. Beat was shocked as three things happened almost simultaneously: a bright flash, a loud bang, and then the engine failed. The boat was at the mercy of the waves, like a nutshell, and threatened to capsize at any moment.

Beat knew they had to act quickly. He grabbed the emergency kit he always had on board and began to make repairs. Jakob and Salome helped him, and eventually, Beat managed to get the engine running again. They crossed the choppy lake slowly.

When they finally reached the harbor, everyone was relieved and grateful they had returned safely.

On the way home, Lisa mentioned an interesting thought that had crossed her mind on the stormy lake. "You were right. You predicted that the return trip to the harbor could be long and dangerous if the storm picked up again. Yet we took the risk, and it became dangerous. I thought that we often find ourselves in such situations in life. We could make ourselves comfortable and postpone a difficult and perhaps unpleasant task for later. But we were ready, and I wouldn't want to miss the experience we had in the past few hours."

"I'm glad you think so positively", Beat replied happily. "I would have blamed myself if something had happened to us. Now, I can only be thankful and happy that we made it and that we stick together when we need each other."

"That's true", said Lisa. "After all, we were literally in the same boat."

Beat was relieved that he could safely guide his family and friends through the storm. He thought of how he had gone fishing on the lake with his father as a little boy. He had never forgotten his dream of owning his own boat and eventually made it come true. Admittedly, he thought, such a boat is a luxury many people cannot afford. And some, who have the money for such a purchase, do not desire to spend it on a gas-guzzling pleasure boat.

What was the fulfillment of a childhood dream for me, my son Flavio may see completely differently. Beat decided to talk to his children about their dreams and wishes at the next appropriate moment.

*After all, everyone has their own dreams...*


**The Wishes of the Three Children**

The opportunity to talk to his children about their biggest wishes came soon.

Beat had promised his daughters Claudia and Conny for their confirmation that each could wish for something unique. Lisa and he would then see what they could do to help fulfill these wishes. "But you may also have to contribute something", he said when they stopped again at the Restaurant Rousseau during a boat trip and sat together at lunch. "And you, Flavio, you're not confirmed yet, but you can also make a wish."

"What do you mean by 'contributing something'?" Claudia wanted to know. "Does that mean we have to pay for part of what we wish for?"

Beat laughed. "No", he said. "But if you're talking about a dream prince you want to marry one day, you have to choose him yourself. If it's material things that make you happy, we can talk about it. So, think about it!"

"Well, that's an offer", replied Claudia. "So, Dad, you've taken me on some motorcycle tours. I loved it, and you've got me interested in racing motorcycles. Maybe I can achieve that, but I'd have to take care of it myself. But I'd love to attend the Moto GP in Italy as a spectator. I'd like to see Valentino Rossi, the best rider in the GP class, live, maybe at the Mugello racetrack near Florence. What do you think?"

"Wow!" exclaimed Flavio. "Not bad!"

Beat was thrilled. "It's booked!" he said, "promised! And you, Conny, what's your wish?"

The younger of the two sisters didn't have to think long. "I want to go to Rio de Janeiro for at least a week. Swim at Copacabana, bike to Ipanema Beach, see a big dance show at Plataforma, and visit the hill with the famous Christ statue. And if possible, I'd like to experience a helicopter tour. And if there's time, I'd love to watch a soccer match at the famous Maracanã Stadium, where Pelé and Maradona once played."

Everyone's eyes widened as they looked expectantly at Beat.

"What do you think, Beat? Are you in?" asked Lisa.

"I think so, I've wanted to go to Brazil for a long time, and if Conny still has the same wish in two years, we'll do it. And now to you, son! You have four years until you can make your wish, but maybe you already have a specific idea…"

Flavio took his time with his wish while everyone waited eagerly. "Yes", said Flavio hesitantly, "but I'm not sure yet. I play for FC Aarberg and sometimes go with you and your clients to YB games in Bern. I like that, and when I'm fifteen, I'd love to be at a top match live. Not in the VIP lounge, but in the middle of the spectators, with the real YB fans."

"Great!" replied Beat. "Let's hope the Young Boys will be playing for the title again in four years!"

"Those are lovely wishes", said Lisa, visibly proud of her children. "Now you're challenged, Mr. Captain!" Laughing, she added, "But first, you must bring us safely back to the harbor without getting us all wet!"


## Knowing Where You Want to Go

Beat's stay at Inselspital is coming to an end. A few more check-ups, then a short rehab. In the last few days, he reached an agreement with his employer. It was a good, open conversation he had with the CEO. They looked forward to Beat's return, his supervisor said, and Beat thanked him for the company's support during his several-month hospital stay. He would gladly resume his work but wanted to use his time at the company to prepare for an early retirement.

Now, he waits in the cafeteria for Phil, with whom he has an appointment. Beat realizes he will miss the regular exchanges with the neurologist as Phil sits down at their table.

"Before I talk about my life again today, I want to change things up and learn more about you", Beat begins the conversation. "Your life must be very interesting, but I know almost nothing about it."

"You're right", Phil agrees. "I'm the professor; you're the patient. I ask questions, you report and hand over documents and records from your life. I'm grateful for that, and your wish to know about my private side is more than justified. Our meetings are no longer comparable to doctor visits, but I must admit, as a researcher in neurology, I am still astonished and delighted at how well you function after your cardiac arrest. I've never seen a patient whose brain went without oxygen for a certain time perform so well."

"I can't explain it myself, but maybe there's no explanation for it..."

"As a scientist, one does not settle for that, of course", Phil says, laughing. "But briefly about myself: I am forty-three, happily married, and have two children. My son Roger is fourteen, and my daughter Sandra is eleven. My wife, Gisela, is three years younger than I am and works part-time in a library."

"So, besides your exciting research work, you are also challenged as a husband and family man — I thought you spent most of your life in the hospital and on research projects."

"Well, there isn't much time left for idleness. Roger will soon be an adult and still doesn't know what he wants to do professionally. He doesn't want to study, anyway. He is also a seeker, similar to how you were at his age. Maybe you'll meet him someday. Sandra is interested in ecological and social issues and has already participated in climate activist demonstrations. In winter, we will take a week of skiing vacation, but the big trips you and Lisa have taken will only be possible for Gisela and me when our children are grown."

"Nice, thanks, Phil. You said your son is also a seeker — what is he looking for?"

"You could say he's missing, quite the opposite of you, a compass. At times he imagines becoming a tour guide, then he thought journalism would be the ideal job for him, and recently he's been toying with the idea of becoming an actor. I'll be surprised by what he thinks of next."

"That might be the problem for many young people today", Beat reflects. "Knowing where you want to go."

"You once asked your children about their wishes", Phil recalls. "What became of that?"

"Each of these wishes was fulfilled. I visited the Italian GP in Mugello with Claudia. She got to visit Valentino Rossi's box and got his autograph. I flew to Brazil with Conny and fulfilled my second eldest daughter's entire wish list in Rio. Flavio is now a member of the YB fan club and knows most of the team's players personally."

"I will also ask Roger and Sandra about their wishes", Phil resolves. "And you? You'll be leaving us soon and re-entering professional life, as I heard. I hope we see each other again before then."

"Certainly, if you have time, I'd love to. After rehab, Lisa and I will first take a vacation and travel to Tenerife."

"That's a good idea. And your book? How are you progressing with it?"

"I'm still sorting through the materials. There are so many travel reports, and I only want to include the most important ones."

"Maybe I'll be inspired by your travel reports; Gisela and I have some catching up to do in that regard", Phil remarks.


## Long Journeys an worldtrips

Beat's dream of traveling to distant lands has come true over the years, and many photo albums and travel reports he has collected are a testament to this.

During his school days, Beat had the desire to discover the world. "When I come of age, I will take long journeys", he told himself. He studied world maps and realized that Switzerland was just a tiny spot on the globe. He read adventure stories set in distant countries and gained an understanding of how many different peoples, cultures, and languages exist on Earth. He was particularly fascinated by Oriental countries, bush, and jungle landscapes.

Each of his trips was a valuable enrichment for him. And he was always aware of where he had come from, often wondering if he wanted to stay where he was at the time. Whether traveling alone or with Lisa, at the end of a tour or a long journey, he was always happy to return to Switzerland.

Beat plans to travel as much as possible in retirement, including to countries he has already visited and wants to see again. But first, he goes through his photo albums and refreshes his memories of previous explorations.

## Dream Destinations

Beat and Lisa married in 1984, and Beat's career had since developed as he had wished. At the age of twenty, he had traveled to Australia with an emigrant visa and stayed there for a year. That time had been formative for him, an episode in his life that he wouldn't want to miss. Since then, he had no longer had emigration plans, but the desire to get to know distant countries remained.

The discovery journeys in the following decades were experienced as tourists, unlike his first stay in Australia, where he had traveled as an emigrant hoping to become rich as a gold and opal seeker.

Beat and Lisa, often with their three children and sometimes with friends, traveled to dream destinations with sandy beaches on the Indian Ocean, wandered through palm forests, and admired the Sigiriya rocks in Sri Lanka, where they visited the sacred mountain Adam's Peak. This mountain, at 2243 meters, is not the highest, but the most significant mountain in Sri Lanka and a pilgrimage site for Buddhists, Hindus, Muslims, and Christians. At the monastery on the summit, there is a 1.8-meter footprint, the Sri Pada, believed by Buddhists to belong to Buddha. Hindus see it as the footprint of the god Shiva, Muslims believe it is Adam's, and Christians think it was left by the Apostle Thomas.

Another spectacular journey was to Ecuador and Cotopaxi, one of the most active volcanoes in the world and, at 5897 meters, the second-highest mountain in the country. In the language of the Incas, Cotopaxi means "Neck of the Moon." On certain nights of the year, the moon can be seen rising directly above the mountain as the "head", illuminating the snow on the summit as a "poncho." No wonder Cotopaxi is also considered a holy mountain.


## The Big Five

In 2008, Beat and Lisa flew with their three children to Nairobi. From there, they traveled by jeep through Nairobi National Park and the next morning to another of Kenya's national parks, Amboseli, with a view of Kilimanjaro, and then on through the Maasai Mara Game Reserve, where they observed elephants, giraffes, lions, buffaloes, zebras, rhinos, and wildebeest. After a week, they arrived at Diani Beach south of Mombasa and stayed at a beach hotel directly on the white sandy beach.

They were deeply impressed to see the wild animals in their natural habitat, and the children wanted to know why the tour guides always referred to the Big Five.

"Which five animals are actually meant by that?" Claudia asked.

Beat had once been interested in this question himself: "I spoke with a Maasai during our tour, and he explained that lions, elephants, rhinos, buffaloes, and leopards are considered the Big Five. The characteristics of these animals are often compared to the different personalities of humans", the Maasai explained, "that is, to the personality of a person."

"Interesting", Claudia remarked. "Which animal would I correspond to, then? Maybe a rhino?"

"Not in appearance, necessarily", laughed Beat. "However, there are two types of rhinos, the black rhino and the white rhino. Based on shape, I'd say you are more like the white rhino."

Claudia threw her empty paper coffee cup at her dad and theatrically pouted.

"No, seriously", Beat continued. "Africans revere these animals: the lion for its strength and loud roar, the elephant for its wisdom and tusks, the rhino for its assertiveness, the buffalo for its aggressive nature, and the leopard as a skilled hunter and for its camouflage."

"Seeing how animals eat each other is brutal", Flavio commented, remembering how they had watched a pack of hyenas devouring the remains of a wildebeest that had presumably been hunted and killed by lions earlier. Nearby, vultures were already eagerly waiting to get their share of the prey.

Beat's thoughts drifted. He recalled how Harry Holzheu had announced at a joint seminar a few years ago that the free market economy functioned according to the same laws as the behavior of predators in the wild: eat or be eaten. It was a constant struggle for survival, both in the animal world and in business and politics. Only humans are equipped with different weapons and abilities than wild predators.

Beat wanted to steer the conversation with his children in a different direction and announced, "I remember a report about the Five-Factor Model that I once read in a book on personality psychology. According to it, the Big Five are a standard model in personality research, with five criteria by which every person can be categorized, such as openness and empathy. But I don't know much more about it. One could also consider the five most important life goals as the Big Five. You could, for example, try to imagine your five life goals that you want to achieve."

"For example, making a lot of money?" Conny asked.

"For that, you'd have to work a lot", Flavio interjected.

Beat saw it differently: "Working a lot doesn't necessarily make you rich. Working to find personal fulfillment", would indeed be a beautiful life goal. And if you also earn enough money in the process, you should consider yourself lucky."

Beat fondly remembered that evening.

In Mombasa, they met Hans Blaser, a Swiss from the Bernese Seeland who had emigrated to Kenya many years ago with his wife. He had built a new life there because he found Switzerland too cramped and cold; he ran a small safari company. Swiss television had recently visited him, and the well-known presenter Mona Vetsch had gone on safari with him and the tour organizer from Let's Go. The documentary, with impressive images, was broadcast on SRF and 3sat.

Hans was always happy to have visitors from Switzerland and was open to a conversation with Beat, who asked him what had prompted him to leave Switzerland.

"Because I felt the need to gain new experiences and develop personally", Hans replied. "I was curious about other cultures and wanted to travel the world. I chose Kenya because I was fascinated by the vastness and beauty of the country and its wildlife."

Hans Blaser was convinced that he had found his new home in Kenya. He had adapted well to the tropical climate and the foreign culture. He had made an effort to learn the local language and make friends with the locals. He now spoke fluent Swahili and had many friends and business partners with whom he got along well. "I don't think I'll ever return to Switzerland for my retirement. Kenya has become my home, and I love living here. I still have many plans, including expanding my safari business and supporting local charitable projects. Every two to three years, I visit my old home in the Bernese Seeland. But I'm content with the decision I made as a young man thirty-five years ago."

Beat thought of his Australian adventure, which had had a significant influence on his later life. Unlike Hans Blaser, he had eventually abandoned his emigration plan and listened to his inner compass. Today, he knows it was right to seek his fortune in Australia and just as right to return to Switzerland.


## Second Trip to Australia after Thirty Years

While sorting through the many records, notes, and photos from previous trips, Beat came across an extensive dossier titled "Second Trip to Australia." He remembered that Phil had been particularly interested in his first trip to Australia, so he decided to take a few pages from the dossier to give Phil at their next meeting.

After five years at Swisscom, Beat was entitled to another sabbatical in January 2010. This meant almost two months of vacation. The decision to visit Australia again after thirty years was quickly made. They were curious about the changes in Down Under and whether Peter Indermühle still lived in the opal field.

The Australian adventure of 1981, with thoughts of emigration, remained a fond memory for Beat and Lisa. That time of gold and opal searching, traveling, working, and living in another culture had shaped them and given them a new foundation for the years after their return to Switzerland.

They booked flights from Zurich with a four-day stopover in Singapore and then to Perth, with the return flight a month later from Sydney. In Perth, a jeep with a built-in roof tent was reserved for them.

In Singapore, they visited some of the city's most famous landmarks: the Merlion, a giant mythical creature with a lion's head and a fish's body; the Marina Bay Sands Skypark, a rooftop garden with an incredible view of the city; Gardens by the Bay, a botanical garden with spectacular artificial trees that light up at night; and the Chinatown district, known for its colorful buildings and traditional markets. Another interesting district was Little India, with its vibrant temples, bustling street markets, and Indian restaurants. They also visited Suntec City, the southernmost point of Asia.

On the fifth day of their journey, Beat and Lisa arrived in Perth, where the reserved jeep awaited them. The first leg of their journey across the entire Australian continent led them to Fremantle, where they visited the historic port and the famous Fremantle Prison. Between 1850 and 1868, England had transferred nearly 10,000 convicts there, who were used as laborers to build roads, bridges, and houses.

At that time, solitary confinement was considered an effective measure for rehabilitating criminals. The prisoners were prohibited from any contact with each other, kept in solitary cells, and totally isolated for several months or even years before they were allowed to contribute to building Australia's infrastructure.

Their journey continued crisscrossing Australia from the Pacific coast to the endpoint Sydney on the Indian Ocean. They made stops in Margaret River, Busselton, Walpole, and the Albany area in southern Western Australia. From there, they traveled northwards on the famous Nullarbor Plain. On Australia's longest straight road, 90 miles (nearly 150 kilometers) without a curve, surrounded on both sides by a barren plain without trees, they drove into the Adelaide area and then towards the Outback to the kangaroos in the Flinders Ranges, known for their spectacular red rocks and gorges. From Coober Pedy, once famous among opal seekers, there were only off-road tracks left, the Strzelecki Track, leading through the Outback landscape. At Cameron Corner, they were at the tri-border area of New South Wales, Queensland, and South Australia.

The Strzelecki Track is named after the Polish explorer Sir Paul Edmund Strzelecki, who traveled with camels in Australia in the 1840s and explored the region. Strzelecki undertook several expeditions to various parts of Australia and became known for his discoveries and explorations, especially in the field of geology. Not to be confused with

John Strelecky, the author of the book "The Café on the Edge of the World." The track was originally a route for cattle drivers and traders transporting goods between South Australia and Queensland. Today, it is popular as a route for adventure tourists wanting to explore the Australian Outback.

From Cameron Corner, it was still about 600 kilometers to White Cliffs in New South Wales. There are still some opal seekers in the area who live in underground dwellings. Beat wanted to find his former Swiss opal and gold mentor, Peter Indermühle.

After a week on dusty and sandy tracks, they saw White Cliffs in the distance. The Outback settlement is 250 kilometers from Broken Hill. Beat remembered how he had helped shear sheep on a farm north of Broken Hill, which was larger than the entire Bernese Seeland, between gold and opal searching, and had been able to earn some money.

"What's it like on such a farm?" Lisa wanted to know.

"On such a large farm in the Australian Outback, various means of transport are often used to herd and care for the sheep. Farmer John owned a small plane, five jeeps, and eight motorcycles to monitor the area and locate the sheep. The motorcycles were used to herd the sheep over the last few kilometers towards the shearing shed, where the shearers awaited them.

Shearing is an important part of the sheep farming industry in Australia. The wool from the sheep is sorted on the farm, packed into bales, and then taken to a wool storage facility, where it is further processed. It can be washed, combed, dyed, and spun into various types of yarn and fabric. Australia is one of the largest wool producers in the world. The quality of the wool depends on many factors, such as the breed of the sheep, its diet, and the type of care it receives. I hope I have answered your question comprehensively enough", said Beat with a grin.

Lisa was impressed: "Yes, thanks for the lecture. And you were one of the shearers?"

"My job was to herd the sheep to the shed on a motorcycle. There, I helped collect the wool and load it onto the truck. In the evening, there was always a big BBQ party. Lamb chops were grilled over the fire, and liters of beer were consumed until some people staggered around before finding somewhere to sleep. But now I'm curious if Peter still lives somewhere in an underground dwelling here."

Beat no longer remembered exactly which of the many hills in the dugout he had stayed with Peter back then. They drove through the settlement, where the pub was on the left and the post office on the right. There was nothing more. Within a three-kilometer radius, you could see the hills where the opal seekers lived in their underground dwellings. There was also an underground bed and breakfast and a campground with a shower and toilets for campers who had made it this far on the other side of White Cliffs. Beat got out at the post office, but no one was to be seen outside in the early afternoon with 35 degrees. Back in the jeep, he said that he felt they might find Peter very close, perhaps one or two kilometers away in a northeastern direction.

"Who's telling you that?" Lisa wanted to know. "Is your compass speaking again?"

"You won't believe it and may laugh at me, but honestly, I feel that Peter is nearby."

Lisa had no idea how one could sense someone who was kilometers away, but she had often experienced that Beat had a kind of special antenna and rarely let his feelings deceive him.

Slowly, Beat steered the jeep over the bumpy road and looked over the opal field with the many hills made by the opal seekers. Intuitively, he directed the jeep fifteen minutes later onto a small driveway towards a hill, where he had spotted a porch and a car at the entrance. He parked up there but saw no one, got out, and went to the entrance with a kind of awning made of tin and wood. Suddenly, he heard voices from outside. He went closer and entered the anteroom. There sat two women and a skinny old man, all holding a cup of tea. Beat greeted them: "Hello and good day. I am looking for Peter Indermühle; do you know where I could find him?"

The three looked at him with wide eyes, then the man stood up and said, "Yes, that's me."

Beat was totally surprised because he hadn't recognized him, without a beard and thirty years older. Once again, he marveled at himself, how his inner compass had led him here to the other side of the world directly to Peter without a phone, internet, or map.

"Tschou Peter, we can speak Swiss German! I'm glad to find you here!"

Peter replied with a broad smile: "Hello, it's great that you came here again... I remember our time well. I'm really happy now!"

Lisa also entered the room, and Beat introduced her to Peter. Conversely, Peter introduced them to the two women, dear neighbors who often visited him while their husbands were searching for gold and opals in the surrounding area. "The good times are over", Peter explained. "The area is almost deserted today."

Then Peter showed them his underground dwelling. Almost everything looked the same as back then. Only over time, the old man had begun to collect and pile up a lot of stuff. His wife and children had left him and now lived in Switzerland. "It doesn't matter", said Peter. "I'm staying here."

Beat soon realized that something wasn't quite right with Peter. The old man pointed with watery eyes up to his hill and explained that he was building a small Italian dome there.

His grave, Beat thought. He saw that Peter had already welded the frame of his dome together from scrap metal. Around it lay things he couldn't or wouldn't part with, junk others had left behind. Beat felt sorry for the old man but could talk with him about past shared experiences, and Peter remembered the young Swiss he had taught gold and opal searching thirty years ago.

*"My compass has led me to nowhere to an old friend. He was like a father to me. I will never forget him."*

*

The next day, Beat planned the trip to Sydney and studied the routes and sights along the way. They were in no hurry and wanted to see as much of this continent as possible. They were also interested in the Aborigines. They lived a totally different life that Beat did not find ideal, but their spirituality and their Song Lines, which he had relied on thirty years ago when he was hopelessly wandering in the Outback, had something mystical.

He noted Australia's sights that they could visit on the way to Sydney:
- The Blue Mountains, a mountain range west of Sydney with the Three Sisters, an impressive rock formation.
- The Jenolan Caves, caves in the Blue Mountains National Park with spectacular underground formations.
- Canberra, Australia's capital, about halfway between White Cliffs and Sydney.
- The South Coast: the coastal region south of Sydney with some of Australia's most beautiful beaches and charming coastal towns.
- The Hunter Valley wine region north of Sydney, known for its wineries and offering a variety of culinary discoveries.
- Newcastle: an industrial city that has developed into an exciting destination in recent years. Not to forget Nobbys Beach and the *Newcastle Art Gallery.*
- The Royal National Park south of Sydney with many hiking trails and spectacular beaches.
- Wollongong: The city is known not only for its beaches and surf scene but also for the *Nan Tien Temple* and the *Wollongong Botanic Garden.*

They set off and drove on the sandy track to Wilcannia. There, Beat showed Lisa where he had waited for two days thirty years ago until a truck driver had taken him to Brisbane. "Near the road by the Murray River, I slept under a tree. I wanted to buy the car and the metal detector in Brisbane before searching for gold."

"And back then, you had the intention to emigrate. I don't know what I would have done, but I'm glad you gave up that plan", Lisa said.

"You're right, but the time without you often made me thoughtful. The questions of life always came in the evenings by the campfire in total solitude: What am I doing here? I want to marry Lisa, start a family, build a house, and find my dream job. Now, thirty years later, almost all my wishes have come true, and I'm happy with you."

While driving, kangaroos hopped over the sandy track, and Beat had to be careful that none jumped in front of the jeep. Lisa, as a hunter's daughter, was very nature-oriented and urged him to drive slower.

"Don't worry, Lisa. I have everything under control. By the way, this evening, when we find a quiet and romantic camping spot off the road, I want to write a longer diary entry. So much has happened that has brought me joy, including things I couldn't have planned in advance. Are you okay with me taking about an hour for my entries in my Gratitude and Success Journal? You know it's become a kind of ritual for me, and today I feel I need my hour again."

"No problem", Lisa replied as they drove towards Sydney, which was still 1500 kilometers away. "I'll prepare our dinner in the bush during that time; we have everything with us."

Twenty minutes later, they found the right spot to camp, and while Lisa began preparing their dinner, Beat discovered a large eucalyptus tree near their jeep, under which he set up the camping table and a chair for his meditation. As if to welcome him, the unmistakable laughter of the kookaburra, the laughing Hans, as Beat called the peculiar bird, sounded.

Beat recorded in his diary everything significant they had seen and experienced since arriving in Perth, supplementing his notes with remarks on thoughts he had had during their journey. He wrote that he felt within himself feelings of love, serenity, wealth, prosperity, peace, joy, confidence, happiness, zest for life, and lightness.

"I continually focus on the feeling of harmony between prosperity and wealth (not just materially) with love", he wrote as his last entry when he heard Lisa calling.

"Beat, hello Beat! Come, dinner is ready. A grilled kangaroo steak and salad are waiting for you!"

The steak tasted excellent. Lisa knew that Beat loved it well-done with no bloody spots left, while she preferred it medium. They talked about the Aborigines, called "Abos" by Australians, and Lisa, who had often gone hunting for foxes, deer, and chamois with her father, wanted to know how they had hunted and killed kangaroos in the past. "Did they use the boomerang as a weapon?"

"Interesting question", Beat said. "But I'm not exactly sure. The boomerang only comes back if it hasn't hit anything. We have some clever books about Australia and the Aborigines with us."

In a book about the culture of the Australian indigenous people, he found answers to Lisa's question.

"There was the kangaroo drive, a group of hunters driving a herd of kangaroos into a bottleneck where they could capture or kill them. There were also kangaroo pits, camouflaged with branches and leaves. Often, kangaroos fell into such traps. Some Aborigines also hunted with bows and arrows or used throwing spears to hunt kangaroos. Indeed, the boomerang is also mentioned, which the hunters used to stun animals they then killed."

The setting sun had now turned the western sky deep red, and the annoying flies had disappeared. "It's amazing how ancient peoples on all continents lived and survived for millennia and until the end of the Middle Ages. Now they are no longer around, and their successors have been relegated to reservations. Is that also in the travel guide?" Lisa asked.

Beat leafed through his books and confirmed to Lisa that the number of Aborigines, estimated at one million people in the mid-18th century, had dropped to about 60,000 by 1920. The known causes were introduced diseases and conflicts with settlers, mainly from Europe, who claimed land rights. "Today, there are supposed to be about 400,000 indigenous people again, three-quarters of whom live in the big cities and have adapted to modern society."

Three weeks later, they reached Sydney, the end of their journey through Australia.


## Last Days in the Hospital

"So, you will be leaving us and resuming your job at Swisscom", Phil remarks after Beat explains that he has agreed with his employer to return as Sales Director. "So, back to business as usual?"

"No", laughs Beat. "Nothing is the same as it was before my cardiac arrest. I'm returning to Swisscom to prepare for my exit from the workforce. I feel that I no longer have the energy to continue this demanding job until retirement."

"Hmm, that seems very sensible. I have to admit, I would be worried if you were to dive back into work full throttle. You know, I am convinced that your cardiac arrest, which struck you like a bolt from the blue, was no coincidence. Unfortunately, the number of patients with acute heart conditions at our hospital has risen sharply in recent years, not to mention the many people who come to us with burnout symptoms."

"Yes, you're right. More and more colleagues, especially those in management positions, are taking early retirement. That used to be the exception; today, it's the rule. A few weeks ago, you said you wanted to find out what might have caused my sudden collapse and cardiac arrest. After all the tests with EKG, EEG, and learning so much about my life, do you have any idea how my blackout happened?"

Beat is still eager to understand how it was possible for him, a healthy and fit person, to narrowly escape death due to a cardiac arrest that seemed to come out of nowhere.

"From a purely medical standpoint, there are no indicators that can definitively explain your cardiac arrest, so all that remains are speculations and hypotheses. However, everything our body does has a cause."

"Do you have a hypothesis in my case?"

"I can try to explain some connections between the brain and the human body", Phil replies thoughtfully. "I might have to delve a bit into technical details."

Beat nods in agreement: "Go ahead, I'm interested."

"I don't want to give a scientific lecture, but I need to provide some background. Many of your actions are conscious: you decide where to look and go, when to say what, and which sounds to focus on. You can control and steer these. Eyes, ears, nose, tongue, and sensors in the skin perceive stimuli from the environment and send them to the central nervous system.

Our nervous system controls the muscles of the organs and regulates vital body functions such as heart activity, breathing, circulation, metabolism, and body temperature. In addition, the nervous system also handles tasks that you do not consciously control. You know this: during sports or stressful situations, your heart rate automatically accelerates, breathing becomes faster, and you start sweating.

The brain is the information center of our body. Here, information from the environment and about the state of the organism is gathered and processed into reactions. The most developed part of the brain is the cerebrum with the cerebral cortex. This is where the processing centers for signals from the eyes, ears, and other sensory organs are located. You probably already know all this.

Other parts of the brain are the diencephalon, midbrain, cerebellum, and medulla. The latter borders the spinal cord and is responsible for the blink reflex, saliva production, as well as sneezing, coughing, and vomiting. It also controls reflexes that ensure we don't fall when stumbling but catch ourselves without much thought. In your case, as we know, this didn't work because you fell uncontrollably and hit your head. Just before that, there must have been a kind of short circuit in your nervous system, and all brain functions were shut down within fractions of a second."

"A short circuit? Like a power outage?"

"Yes, that's a fair comparison. The human nervous system consists of countless nerve cells — we speak of many billions — that constantly receive signals and pass them on to other nerve cells or muscle and gland cells. Signals are transmitted electrically along a nerve cell. The speed of these signals reaches up to 360 km/h. These speeds are necessary because, for example, signals must travel a relatively long distance from the brain to the leg muscles. The contact point between two nerve cells is the synapse. Here, the transmission of the electrical signal from one nerve cell to the next occurs with the help of messenger substances, also known as transmitters. The function of the brain and nervous system is based on both the transmission of electrical signals and biochemical processes. Often, the causes of neurological and psychiatric disorders lie in a disturbance of biochemical signal transmission."

"Quite complex. So, did my collapse have something to do with the processing of such signals?"

"Maybe — really just maybe, because I don't want to make any assertions — your nervous system experienced a sensory overload. This can lead to the brain releasing too many messenger substances and being unable to process all these stimuli. We cannot reconstruct the scene; your memories of what happened immediately before your cardiac arrest are erased anyway. I suggest we consider this possibility and leave it at that for now."

"It's true that about four days are erased from my memory; I can't remember how I drove to Tenero and checked into the hotel. I will think about your hypothesis that sensory overload in the nervous system could have been the cause. And I am very grateful for the time you've taken for all these conversations with me."

"Well, you will have to come by occasionally for routine check-ups, and I would be happy if we could meet for discussions during such visits. I'm also interested in how you are progressing with your book."

"I will continue working on it. But first, I have to complete the last days of rehab and then go on a holiday trip with Lisa. You'll hear from me."

Four months after his cardiac arrest, Beat wrote in his Gratitude and Success Journal that he felt healthy.


## One year later

In the summer of 2020 — Beat had been back at work for a few months — he ran the eight kilometers in Tenero in good health, following the same route where his life had nearly ended a year earlier. People from the Federal Office of Sport recognized him immediately and still remembered the incident that had led to the cancellation of the Swisscom Games.

Back in Lyss, on June 21, Beat invited guests to a BBQ to commemorate and express gratitude. Among the guests were CEO Urs Schaeppi, Thomas Marfurt, and Stefan Kilchenmann. Urs Lehner, who had been the head of the business customer segment and was present at the incident the previous year, showed Beat photos of the accident site in Tenero and the Rega helicopter that had found a landing spot on the golf course.

From Thomas, his lifesaver, Beat learned what had happened that day: "As the golf tournament was progressing slowly, my colleagues and I were waiting on a bench before we could continue on hole 13. The path where other athletes were jogging ran right through the golf course. I watched as you ran towards us, and together we cheered you on. You seemed pleased, but the exertion and some fatigue were visible. Suddenly, you started to stagger and looked for support. Apparently, you lost consciousness, fell backward onto the road, and hit your head on the hard asphalt. The fall was shocking, and I rushed to you immediately. You were lying motionless on the ground, and I shouted to my colleagues to get help.

You were unresponsive, your eyes wide open. For a moment, I thought you were dead, but I forced myself to stay calm and not panic. Every second counted now. I turned you on your back and immediately started life-saving measures as I had learned in a first aid course. Meanwhile, I shouted for a defibrillator. After what felt like five minutes, a paramedic arrived and offered to take over the chest compressions. Next, a police car with two officers arrived. The officers prepared everything to use the defibrillator on you. Shortly after, we heard the rescue helicopter searching for a suitable landing spot."

Beat was glad to finally learn the details of the incident that had nearly led to his death a year ago. The cause of his cardiac arrest will probably always remain a mystery to him, but he knows he will be forever grateful to Thomas for acting so quickly and effectively.

# Back to Work

After three months of intensive rehabilitation, Beat was ready to return to work. During his absence, his colleague Marc had excellently filled his role as Sales Director at Swisscom. This allowed Beat to resume his position smoothly.

Now, he sits in the CEO's office discussing his desire for early retirement. They reach an agreement acceptable to both sides: on April 25, 2022, Beat's 62nd birthday, he can begin early retirement. This gives him six months to find a successor, both internally and externally. A termination agreement is drafted, stipulating that Beat will mentor and introduce his successor for three months.

After an intensive search, an internal employee is finally selected as his successor: Daniel, a leader who is already well-acquainted with Swisscom's corporate culture. Together, Beat and Daniel focus on the public sector customer segment and design an engaging onboarding phase. In client meetings and with department heads and specialists, Beat introduces Daniel as the new key contact.

## Memories of Highlights

After 32 years, during which Beat had risen to the executive levels of the country's largest telecommunications company, he faces his exit from professional life with mixed feelings. He looks forward to early retirement but is also aware that he will be shedding a heavy load of responsibility and saying goodbye to many cherished colleagues.

He often reflects on the early years of his career and marvels at how technological developments over the past decades have fundamentally changed communication behavior. Artificial intelligence has become a major topic, and he wonders how much AI will eventually change society. Certain questions, such as the meaning of life, will still need to be answered individually by everyone. He looks forward to having more time to devote to subjects and questions that concern him.

In his various roles as Head of Distribution and Key Account Management and later as one of the Sales Directors at Swisscom, Beat inevitably had many contacts with personalities from business, politics, media, and television. He remains in contact with many of them, and some of these acquaintances have turned into friendships that he will continue to nurture in retirement. Planning his time after leaving professional life already occupies much of his thoughts. Being indispensable to the employer was always something he took for granted. Now, as he prepares to say goodbye to his colleagues, he is convinced that the company will function well without him. This gives him a good feeling.

In the last six weeks before his departure, he is still working part-time as a consultant and coach. Two weeks before his final workday, Daniel requests a meeting.

"Beat, you have to help me!" Daniel begins. "We want to give you a dignified send-off, and you must realize that after more than thirty years in a senior position in our company, you can't just slip out quietly through the back door", he says with a grin.

"What do you have planned? There's no need to put on a fireworks display for me", Beat replies.

"Why not?" Daniel laughs. "No, but it's a special occasion, and I've been given the task of moderating it. But that's not so easy. I know that you've experienced countless exciting moments in your job, which you could probably talk about for hours. I've received some information from HR, just the usual stuff, nothing really personal. So my request is: could you write down some notes or anecdotes from your experiences that stand out in your memory?"

"Hmm... you're right, there's a lot to choose from. I'll make you a deal: I'll write down what comes to mind, and you can pick out what you think is funny or interesting enough to be mentioned. Is that okay with you?"

Daniel is relieved. "Great. Don't stress yourself over it!"

Actually, a nice task, Beat thinks, and a kind gesture from the company to give a longtime employee a nice send-off. And poor Daniel is worried that compiling my anecdotes might stress me out. It really is time to go.

Three days later, Beat hands his successor a folder with fifty pages of handwritten notes and documents. "Pick out what you want! You won't need everything, otherwise, the audience will fall asleep."

"Wow!" Daniel exclaims. "You could make a book out of this."

"You have to estimate what can fit into about ten minutes of speaking time. I wouldn't want to bore the audience for longer than that. People are mostly looking forward to the reception afterward", Beat advises.

That means overtime, Daniel sighs as he starts to delve into Beat's documentation.


## At the Right Time, in the Right Place

Throughout his life, Beat has met many people, both privately and professionally, who are well-known throughout Switzerland and sometimes beyond. For his departure from professional life, he handed over several anecdotes about such encounters to Daniel, knowing that not everything can be detailed at a farewell party due to time constraints. He left it to his successor to pick a few highlights.

### Thanks to Thomas

Being in the right place at the right time often has a lot to do with luck, but it can sometimes be crucial for the course of a life. When Beat looks back on his more than thirty years of professional life, he first sees himself in 1990 as an employee at the General Directorate of PTT, the Swiss Postal, Telegraph and Telephone Service. In 1997, after the new Postal Organization Act (POG) and the new Telecommunications Act (TUG) came into force, the Swiss telecommunications market was deregulated. The Swiss Post received the legal form of a public institution, and Swisscom emerged after this division in October of the same year as a corporation that was then partially privatized.

In 1994/95, Beat was responsible for setting up and organizing the Sales and Marketing division for the international company Unisource Business Network, which was then partly owned by Telecom. As such, he was responsible for handling business with the three most important major customers, one of which was ABB in Baden. After his later switch to Swisscom, he was able to train Thomas Marfurt as his successor for the care of ABB. It was the same Thomas who, eight years later, performed the first life-saving measures when Beat suffered his cardiac arrest in Tenero. Without his quick intervention, Beat wouldn't be here today. It was Thomas who was in the right place at the right time.

## The Watch King

In the mid-1990s, when Beat was already head of the Data Networks division at the Telecom General Directorate, turbulent times were on the horizon. In the early 1990s, European telecom companies were still "friends" and regularly met for coordinated knowledge exchange. There was active work on the coordinated introduction of a cross-border ISDN strategy. Beat always attended these meetings as an assistant to the elected chairman Pierre Lässer. Pierre was also his team leader in Switzerland and needed an assistant who could speak English and relieve him of technical and organizational tasks. So Beat traveled weekly from Norway to Cyprus and from Hungary to Ireland to all European countries.

But as the liberalization wave slowly gained momentum, the international marketing group of telecom experts was dissolved, and privately organized companies became competitors.

A new challenging time began. The Telecom PTT had also reoriented and reorganized itself. Customers no longer simply ordered according to a tariff list, but for larger orders, a quote had to be prepared in advance. The Telecom Consulting division was established, and consultants were trained to become key account managers. Beat could learn a lot of new things and develop further.

Now the big customers who bought many data network services demanded a contact person who, if necessary, would submit a corresponding offer with a team.

The international watch company Swatch Group, with brands like Omega, Rado, Blanchpain, Breguet, Longines, and many others, had a great need to network their factories, locations, and partners around the world.

At such customers, it was Beat's task to prepare the so-called executive meetings between the presidents/CEOs and coordinate them with the staff departments and purchasing.

Beat had prepared everything and traveled with the then Telecom boss Tony Reis to the well-known watch king Nicolas G. Hayek in Biel. They were received personally by Patron Hayek on the top floor. First, there was friendly presidential small talk before getting down to business. Hayek and Reis agreed that the new liberalization in the global telecom market would have positive effects for all parties involved.

Beat behaved rather reserved during this conversation, in active listening mode. But then suddenly Hayek looked Beat directly in the eyes, paused, and asked him: "What do you think about the current business situation and the network services we are now and in the future buying and operating for our international network?"

Diplomatically and with a smile, Beat replied that the general situation was developing positively, but there was a business situation that worried him.

Hayek, direct and authentic as he was known, immediately said: "Then please tell me what worries you!"

Beat's boss widened his eyes but waited eagerly for his assistant's response.

Beat didn't have to think long and surprised his superior: "Two months ago, the Swatch Group's purchasing department and their IT experts asked how their new global data network could be expanded. Telecom PTT made an offer, and we received feedback that the competing offer from France Telecom Global One was cheaper and better. That is the reason for my concern."

Hayek furrowed his thinker brow and said he had no knowledge of this business. But he would inquire immediately. Spontaneously, as was typical for him, he picked up the receiver of his comfort device and asked his assistant to get the head of purchasing on the phone. After a minute, he was on the line, and Hayek asked him about the status of the negotiations with the telecom partner for their new global data network.

What exactly was said, Beat and Tony Reis didn't hear. But they heard Hayek at the end of the conversation instructing the head of purchasing to wait with signing the contract with France Telecom until he personally gave the okay. Swiss Telecom would submit a new offer, and only then would a decision be made.

That was a clear announcement, and Tony Reis got a chance to keep the prestigious international business in Switzerland after all. Hayek only mentioned that he would like to receive this new offer soon and that he always chose a Swiss company if it could compete with the competition. "I am also a Swiss", he said.

Beat was not only in the right place at the right time but also seized the opportunity that presented itself.

*If you have a trump card, use it at the right moment! If you recognize advantages for both sides in a negotiation, you can convince with arguments.*

Beat and Tony Reis were amazed at how important decisions were made patriarchally by the top boss in this large international watch company. But for them, it was positive, and they took the new opportunity. After submitting an optimized offer, they received the lucrative order from the Swatch Group.

When the new network went live worldwide a year later, visits to the Swatch Group's locations in Canada, the USA, Asia, and the Far East were requested. Beat, along with those responsible for the installation and commissioning of the global data network, made these visits.

A few years later: Telecom/Swisscom organized three to four sales and marketing meetings per year in all parts of Switzerland. Customers were often invited to share their experiences with Telecom/Swisscom directly.

When Beat was asked by the event organization if a personality from business or politics in the Bern/Biel region would be willing to appear and share their experiences, he suggested asking Nicolas Hayek. The organization and management agreed and tasked Beat with directly contacting Hayek with his proposal.

The patron of the Swatch Group promptly agreed to appear in the auditorium of the new Telecom/Swisscom building. The announcement of the watch king's appearance caught the media's attention. Swiss television also wanted to cover the event and feature it on the evening news.

Beat had the task of preparing this appearance with Hayek and his management team. Dutifully, he accepted the task but first had to get Hayek's okay because the television would be involved. In a conversation with the entrepreneur, he agreed, but on the condition that Beat would accompany him from the Swatch headquarters to the Swisscom building, which was a kilometer away. Fulfilling this request, Beat accompanied the Swatch patron on his walk through the city center. Hayek's unassuming manner of interacting with people on the street impressed Beat.

They reached the Telecom/Swisscom building without incident, where Hayek was expected by a hundred sales experts, sales directors, and of course the then Swisscom boss Tony Reis. The television and many journalists were present.

## The Lottery Business

In 1999, when Swisscom took on the challenge of networking all 3,500 kiosks in Switzerland with data services, the lottery industry was still in the era of manual ticket issuance. Paper forms from all over Switzerland had to be mailed to the central lottery office, where they were processed and winners determined.

The Swiss Financial Market Supervisory Authority (FINMA) set strict requirements for accepting money, and a secure digital solution had to be found to ensure that lottery tickets could be reliably filled out and submitted. Beat's spontaneous idea to apply for a banking license for Swisscom was rejected by CEO Jens Alder to avoid conflicts with major banks.

Beat then proposed solving the problem with the help of Blue Window and its founder Peter Rudin. Peter was brought onto the project team and presented possible ways to achieve digitalization.

**Peter Rudin:**

"You have to think big! You won't succeed on the Internet if you think in small dimensions. You have to be number one, two, or three. And if you think big, you need big money."

The 59-year-old Swiss Peter Rudin knows what he's talking about. The former manager took 14 years of apprenticeship before he dared to go public. This August, his company UPAQ is set to launch as a corporation - his business: electronic commerce. His goal: revenues in the hundreds of millions. From small entrepreneur to medium-sized business: Peter Rudin found a springboard for his late entrepreneurial career with the Internet.

From the archives of Deutschlandfunk, March 12, 2000

Finally, in March of the following year, the contract was signed. This laid the foundation for the digitalization of Swisslos in Basel, which is now eighty percent digital. Blue Window no longer exists since 2005, but Swisscom continues to use the brand name "bluewin" as its email platform.

Because Beat was responsible for Swisscom's business with Swiss television and the lottery business for the "Benissimo" show, he came into contact with various well-known SRF actors. Beat and his wife were often invited to the show by the then director of Swisslos, Dieter Ryffel, and were able to watch the show live in Studio 1, observing the popular host Beni Thurnheer ("Beni national") as he took calls from TV viewers who could choose one of the colored balls containing great prizes.

## The Weather Roof on Top oft the TV Building in Zurich

For the meteorologists who present the weather forecasts after the "Tagesschau", Swiss television came up with something special: the weather roof. Located at the top of SRF's high-rise building, the weather presenters are exposed to rain, snow, and wind. SRF Meteo became one of the most popular shows on Swiss television.

During his visits to SRF, Beat had several opportunities to visit the weather roof with Sandra Boner and Christoph Siegrist. He remains friendly with Sandra to this day. They both fondly remember a Thuner-see event where Swisscom had invited large customers to a symposium, traveling by ship from Interlaken to Thun. Sandra Boner, the weather fairy, was supposed to entertain the guests by explaining the local weather situation live.

"You are a sporty woman. Could you give your forecast while doing a headstand and in high waves?"

"Why not?" Sandra laughed. "I can try!"

And she did it with aplomb, and the guests were thrilled.

At another Swisscom symposium, Swiss television's Kurt Aeschbacher explained to the exclusive guests on the steamship "Blümlisalp" what they would see in five minutes from the ship. Aeschbacher's task was to lead the event's moderation in an entertaining way.

As the ship set off, Aeschbacher pointed to a car on the shore. Over the loudspeaker, he announced that Frank Rinderknecht from Rinspeed would show everyone how a car could drive from the road onto the lake and become a boat. It felt like a James Bond movie. Agent 007 had also shown how he dives into the water with a car and then drives back onto the beach. When emerging from the water, Roger Moore as James Bond had thrown a fish, which had somehow gotten into the car, back into the sea.

The car slowly drove into the lake, and after a few meters, it floated on the water like a boat. Frank Rinderknecht waved out the window to the laughing and applauding people on the ship. A cheerful mood set in as the "Blümlisalp" headed towards Thun, where the gala dinner was planned. Frank Rinderknecht drove the car back to shore and then to Thun on the road to attend the evening event.


## Emotional Selling

In the age of digitalization, a telecom company is particularly challenged to not only keep up with the competition when introducing new technologies but to take a leading role. This is partly a question of technical competence in product development and partly a question of social competence in marketing.

While browsing for literature on social competence, Beat came across the books "Emotional Intelligence" by Daniel Goleman and "Winning Trust" by Harry Holzheu (†). Both write about emotional competence and emotional intelligence (EQ), and both agree that EQ is at least as important as IQ for successful marketing strategies.

This resonated with Beat, who has always successfully relied on his inner compass when making important decisions. He found confirmation of what he had always believed.

Holzheu was internationally known as a business consultant; at that time, Beat was the head of a sales team in Basel and Biel. He was looking for a coach who could competently convey Holzheu's theories. Why not ask Holzheu directly if he was interested? His clients included world-renowned companies like ABB, the Federal Government, the Army, ETH, Bosch, UBS, Daimler-Chrysler, lottery companies, IBM, and Nestlé.

Beat attended one of Holzheu's lectures and knew afterward that he was the right coach for his team. Beat's proposal was approved. After coordinating schedules and preparing training rooms in Basel and Bern, they were ready to start. Beat and Holzheu developed a seminar booklet for the participants. They chose a simple title: "Those Who Can't Smile, Can't Do Business. Emotional Selling."

The course participants were enthusiastic. Harry Holzheu and his convincing way of imparting knowledge were highly motivating and unforgettable.

Beat remained in contact with Harry Holzheu for a long time, who passed away in September 2021.

## Artificial Intelligence

In the last years of his professional life, Beat, as the person responsible for large customers at the telecom company, observed an accelerated development in the application of artificial intelligence in areas that had previously been managed by highly qualified and specialized individuals. It's no longer just about sorting, packaging, and shipping products but about computer-controlled strategies and decisions.

Today, computer programs can beat the world's best chess players and translate long texts from one foreign language into any other language in seconds.

Beat also had his first experiences with Chat GPT and was impressed by the quick and precise answers to the questions he had asked the program.

Whether artificial intelligence exists can be recognized by the fact that a questioner cannot tell whether a human or a machine is formulating the answers.

Self-Driving Cars

Beat had invited several politicians (members of the National and Council of States) with Stefan Kilchenmann to prepare them for the new self-driving cars. In May 2015, the first converted car, a VW Passat, was to be provided by the company Autonomos in Berlin and tested on Zurich's streets. This required an exceptional permit from the Federal Department of the Environment, Transport, Energy, and Communications (UVEK), which Beat prepared in many discussions and which was eventually signed by the then Federal Councillor Doris Leuthard.

From May 4 to 14, the car self-drove through the city of Zurich for test drives. For safety, specialists who could intervene in an emergency sat behind the wheel. "I was thrilled with yesterday's drive", said Swisscom's CEO Christian Petit.

Technically, autonomous driving is possible today, but the technology on the part of car manufacturers and the legal situation on the part of legislation are more complex than expected. "It will still take years before self-driving cars are approved for our roads", Beat learned from an expert at Autonomos.

AI in Everyday Life

In conversations with IT experts and decision-makers in business and politics about the possibilities of future AI applications in industrial production and the service sector, Beat got an idea of how automation processes will increasingly change our private lives and jobs in the coming years.

Even in his immediate work environment, Beat was confronted with AI: Sam, the digital assistant in the Data Analytics and AI department, ensures that conversations with customers run as naturally as possible, around the clock and regardless of the channel – be it by phone, chat, email, or a good old-fashioned letter.

**Stephen Hawking (†):**
Whether machines will eventually take over control will be revealed by the future. What is already clear today: machines will increasingly displace humans from the job market.

*

After a beautiful and fitting farewell party in a smaller circle at the end of April 2022, and after 32 years at Telecom, Unisource, and Swisscom, Beat ended his exciting career at the age of 62.

# The Compass of Life

Beat and Lisa have just returned from a vacation in Egypt. At Zurich Airport, Lisa reminds him, "Don't forget you have an appointment at Inselspital the day after tomorrow!"

"I know", Beat replies. "The usual check-ups. I'll ask Phil if we can meet for coffee afterward."

Since Beat retired, he and Phil have been meeting every few months.

## The Factor of Chance

The two greet each other in the cafeteria of Inselspital like old friends. "I need to get used to this wet and cold weather again", Beat laughs as they sit down. "But I'm optimistic that the check-ups this morning went well. Have you heard anything about the results?"

"Yes, you don't need to worry. ECG, EEG, blood pressure, blood lipids, cholesterol, ultrasound: all normal. You're a lucky guy", Phil grins.

"That's good to hear. I've been so lucky in life that I sometimes wonder if it's all just chance or if it has something to do with my belief in the law of attraction. What do you think as a scientist?"

"You're asking questions that aren't easy to answer", Phil smiles, taking a sip of his double espresso. "I've read your life story, and you mention this law of attraction several times. Of course, neurologists like me and especially psychologists deal with this topic, and there are countless books in the esoteric literature that often become bestsellers. But if you ask me: As a scientist, I wouldn't call it a law, more of a principle. Yes, it's proven that a positive attitude towards solving a problem is more likely to lead to success than a skeptical or negative mindset. This has been demonstrated in many studies."

"So, you also believe that positive thinking attracts luck and success, right?"

"Basically, yes, but you can't automatically achieve luck and success just by being positive and constantly wishing for good things. That would be too simple and naive. But you can influence luck and chance a bit."

"What do you mean by that? Manipulation?"

"I'll give you an example. A colleague of mine, Professor Christian Busch from New York University, also a neurologist, recently told me about studies on chance. He mentioned an experiment conducted by British psychologists with people who considered themselves either lucky or unlucky. They selected a subject from each group and gave them a simple task: walk down the street and sit in a café at the end. What they didn't tell the subjects: there were hidden cameras along the way and in the café. They placed a bill on the ground just before the café. Inside, there was only one free seat at a table with a successful businessman."

"Interesting. What happened?"

"The lucky person walked down the street, saw the bill, picked it up, and looked around. No one else seemed to care. He went into the café, asked the businessman if the seat was free, and started a conversation. Soon they exchanged business cards."

"And the unlucky person?"

"He walked the same path, didn't see the bill, and sat next to the businessman in the café without speaking to him. That was it. When asked how their day went, the lucky person said: Great, I found a bill on the street and met an interesting person. The unlucky person said: Nothing happened today."

Beat grinned. "A nice example. Awareness and openness are good prerequisites for recognizing opportunities when they present themselves."

"Exactly. We differentiate between blind luck and active luck. You can't influence blind luck, like the lottery draw or the family you're born into; that's social injustice. Active luck is the interplay between chance and human action. It depends on whether you're receptive to a chance discovery that you can use to your advantage."

*Active luck: the ability to be open to unexpected discoveries without actively forcing them.*

"In your notes and reports, I found several examples where you literally stumbled upon such opportunities", Phil says. "For instance, during your apprenticeship, when you struck up a conversation with a secretary who gave you her brother's address, who was searching for gold in Australia. That was the impetus for your first adventure. Or your first encounter with Nicolas Hayek, where you made the right comment at the right moment, leading the watch company executive to give you a major contract. All pure chance?"

"No", Beat replies. "I explained such occurrences to myself with the law of attraction. Positive thinking, you know?"

"I understand. Call it what you will. It makes me think of a challenging case we have, a burn-out patient."

Phil looks up at the ceiling, seeming to ponder how to continue.

"How challenging?" Beat asks cautiously.

"Well, we increasingly have more patients with burn-out symptoms for whom we offer various therapies. Mostly, we have positive experiences and can help the affected individuals step by step out of their low points. It takes time and patience from both sides. We know much more today about the causes and effects of such illnesses and generally find the right methods that the patients respond to."

"But not always, apparently. You mentioned a challenging case..."

"Right. An intelligent man, born in 1962, so two years younger than you. You might even know him..."

"Hmm... unlikely. Why do you think so?"

"His name is Markus Hofmann, a Bernese who emigrated to India about forty years ago – to Goa. He returned to Switzerland five years ago, looking for work and struggling to adjust. In your travel descriptions, I read about a Markus you met on your India trip."

Beat touches his forehead and closes his eyes for a moment. Markus Hofmann? He can't remember the last name, but he recalls a Markus with whom he philosophized about God and the world in Goa. "Yes, maybe", he says hesitantly.

"Here we are again with chance. You could meet him if you're interested. But don't feel obligated; perhaps it's all a mistake, and the man isn't the one you met over thirty years ago."

"I'm happy to do you the favor", Beat replies. "But please don't expect me to come as a therapist or pull something out of a hat to lift this Markus out of his low."

"Thank you, Beat. I appreciate that and will leave it to chance how Markus reacts. Do you have a few more minutes? The man is sitting over there at the table, waiting for a conversation with me, which I scheduled for three this afternoon in the cafeteria. Sorry to spring this on you, but the idea of introducing you just came to me. You can still decline to participate spontaneously."

Beat is taken aback and unsure whether to be annoyed or spontaneously accept Phil's suggestion. "That's pretty sly of you", he says, finally laughing. "I think you're making me a test subject in one of your experiments. But fine! I'll go along with your attempt!"

Markus is busy reading the "Berner Zeitung" and looks up, surprised, at the two men approaching his table. "Uh, hello, Mr. Koch", he says, then scrutinizes the man standing next to the professor.

Phil shakes his hand and introduces him to Beat: "Beat Bongni was a long-term patient here at Inselspital after an accident two years ago, and we've been meeting here in the cafeteria from time to time since then. During our conversations, we talked about his past travels, and I learned that he visited India over thirty years ago, around the time you had been living in Goa for a while. Since Beat is here and I happen to have a meeting with you today, I thought it might be interesting to introduce you two."

He looks at Beat and says, "Beat, this is Markus Hofmann, who emigrated to India forty years ago and is now trying to get back on his feet in Switzerland."

Beat greets Markus with a broad grin. "Hello Markus, nice to meet you. I'm not sure if we've met before..."

Beat doubts whether the man in front of him is the same Markus he philosophized with in Goa years ago. Markus's robust build and broad shoulders in the hippie style are long gone. Markus's hair is gray and short, and the black-rimmed glasses with tinted lenses make him look a few years older than he is, Beat thinks.

"Hello Beat. Um, I'm not sure if we've met either", Markus replies uncertainly.

"The mid-80s", Beat prompts. "Lisa, my wife, was also there."

"Oh, yes, I vaguely remember. You were tourists, and you wanted to know why I emigrated to India."

"Right. You said back then that Switzerland had become too cramped for you, you were fed up with the narrow-mindedness and materialism of the Swiss, and you found happiness and a fulfilling life in India. Why, if I may ask, did you come back?"

"That's a long story. Have you been back to India since then?"

Beat shakes his head.

"Society has changed drastically in the last thirty years, especially in India. The gap between poverty and wealth has always been significant in India; now, it's enormous. The materialism you mentioned is just as widespread in India as it is here. When I gradually ran out of money, I had practically no choice but to return home. As a broke foreigner, you have little chance in India."

"And then? You were a banker, if I remember correctly."

"Exactly. After returning to Switzerland, I became a 'Bünzli' again and applied for a job at Credit Suisse, where I had completed my apprenticeship, and got a trial job as an investment advisor. It was a bad decision to re-enter that business. Encouraging investors to take risks and downplaying or concealing those risks just isn't my thing. I became depressed and fell ill. Because I had debts, I took stimulants and tried to get through the workday, but it didn't get any easier as CS slid from one crisis to another and the atmosphere among colleagues became increasingly tense.

Before the UBS takeover of CS, I had a breakdown; nothing worked anymore. I still don't know exactly what happened. A colleague called emergency services – supposedly, I was found unconscious on the floor at my workplace – and when I came to, I was lying in a bed at Inselspital."

"It was a heart disorder as a result of total emotional exhaustion", adds Phil.

"I'm very sorry to hear that", Beat says sympathetically. "How are you now?"

"Physically, somewhat okay; the doctors here do a good job. But I feel incapable of re-entering the workforce, and I don't want to live on social assistance. I need to find a job just to pay off my debts.

To return to Switzerland, find an apartment, pay health insurance premiums, and cover living expenses, I had to take out a loan. Even with social assistance, I wouldn't get back on my feet, so I need to find a job. But who hires a sixty-year-old with my background? All the therapy for my self-esteem feels wasted, and sending out futile job applications is just humiliating."

"I understand. But can you imagine a job that you'd find interesting and meaningful? Something that matches your skills? Just imagine for a moment that age, applications, and finances don't matter!"

Markus looks at Beat, bewildered, and theatrically throws up his hands. "Are you kidding? What good would that do? What good are such fantasies to me?"

Ignoring the dismissive gesture, Beat asks, "What languages do you speak? How did you communicate all those years in India?"

"Mostly in English. In Goa, they speak Konkani, which I learned over time. I also understand Tamil fairly well. But that's only spoken in South India and Sri Lanka; no one here cares about that."

"I see it differently", Beat replies. "Are you aware that about 60,000 Tamils live in Switzerland?"

"No. You mean...?"

"I mean you have good chances of finding a job that you're good at and might enjoy. Have you heard of a free trade agreement that Switzerland is trying to conclude with India?"

Markus shakes his head.

"I know people in parliament working on this agreement. And I can imagine that someone with your background could be very interesting to them. India is the most populous country in the world and a significant trading partner for Switzerland."

"You mean...?"

"Yes, I mean. And I mean you should think about it. Here's my card, and if you decide to pursue it, let me know, and I can knock on the relevant doors."

Markus can hardly believe it. "Incredible. I wouldn't even know how to thank you if something came of it. And whether I'd have the strength and ability to try something completely new again."

"You can. But think about it for a week before letting me know."

After saying goodbye to Markus and walking with Phil towards the cafeteria exit, the neurologist says, "That was wonderful. I just saw Markus Hofmann smile for the first time. What do you call what you just did in your jargon? Manifesting?"

"Basically, yes. You just have to be able to set aside everything negative and focus on the positive, on what you want and believe is possible."


## The Art of Manifestation

Later that evening, after Beat's encounter with his old acquaintance Markus Hofmann, Phil calls him. He thanks Beat again for being willing to talk to Markus on such short notice. "After you left and I went back to Markus's table, he asked me what I thought about your idea regarding the India project and if your suggestion was serious."

"Of course I meant it seriously, but I understand why Markus is uncertain. I'd feel the same in his position."

"I understand that too. Markus is in a downward spiral from which he can't find a way out without external help. Our experienced therapists haven't managed to lift him up. Then you came along and in a short time managed to spark his interest in something new for the first time. And that after saying you couldn't pull anything out of a hat. You even surprised me."

"I'm glad he's interested in my suggestion. But concretely, we haven't achieved anything yet. Manifestation is more complex than it looks and than some people believe. Manifestation is the realization and experience of using one's own creative power. It's the ability to pre-experience a fulfilled wish with our imagination. There's no guarantee of success. First, someone with a problem must be able to temporarily block out their biggest worries. If you can't do that, you'll always end up at the same intersection that leads downward. Second, you need to have a success goal and be convinced you can handle the new tasks that come with achieving that success goal. That's not simple either; some people constantly overestimate themselves or have too little self-confidence."

"That sounds reasonable", Phil says.

"Third: If you're in a downward spiral, you must be willing to accept external help. No one can pull themselves out of a mess by their own hair."

*A downward spiral acts like a vortex that pulls you down. You need external help to get back up.*

"You can tell all this to Markus. He should take a week before getting back to me. I need to feel that he's truly determined to take the first step before I contact people who might be interested in meeting him. And one more thing: When I say that you have to block out your biggest worries while manifesting, I don't mean you should ignore or suppress your problems. Instead, you need to mentally clear away obstacles to make room for new ideas. Only then can you start seeing problems as tasks you can solve, one by one."

"Thank you, Beat. I agree with everything you said, and I will talk to Markus."

A week later, Markus contacted Beat and said he had decided to seize his opportunity and apply for an interesting job. Beat promised to look around and contacted Sven Medard, who held a senior position in the Department of Economic Affairs, Education and Research (WBF). Beat had met Sven when it came to outsourcing a large IT project by Swisscom to India. Sven confirmed that he was involved in the free trade agreement project with India and that he would like to meet Markus. "People with a Swiss passport and so much experience in India are not easy to find", he confirmed.

*

A few days later, Beat meets with Markus and Phil in the Inselspital cafeteria. He explains what he discussed with Medard and waits eagerly for Markus's reaction.

"I'm looking forward to the meeting with Mr. Medard", Markus says. "I'm a bit nervous and not sure if I can meet the WBF's expectations."

"I'm convinced you're the right man for the job", Beat replies calmly. "Just listen to what it's about and what your role would be. If you believe you can handle it, you'll get the job. It's crucial that you believe in yourself. Stand in front of a mirror at home, look at yourself, straighten up, smile, and say to yourself, 'I can do this!' You'll see that it makes a positive difference."

Markus looks up and smiles. "I know what you mean. You're right, I need that conviction that I'm not a failure. I know the mirror trick and can confirm that I've struggled lately to accept the person I see."

All formalities are discussed, and Markus knows where to report. He stands up, thanks Phil and Beat for their support, and leaves.

"That was brief", Phil says. "No big discussions, not many questions—do you think Markus will take the decisive step now?"

"Yes, I have a good feeling."

"I have to admit", Phil says, "your method of manifestation seems to resonate well with Markus. You've given him a new perspective, a goal that doesn't seem unrealistic."

"Manifestation doesn't mean you can cross your arms and wait for a wish to be fulfilled without doing anything. You have to regularly, if possible daily, engage with the law of attraction and learn to handle it. Whether Markus can give his life new meaning in the long term, I don't know and can't influence. It depends on him whether he seizes his opportunity."

"I agree", Phil says. "Everyone has wishes, and it's just a small step to imagine what it would be like if a special wish came true and changed everything for the better. But there's a big difference between wanting to be healed from an illness and wishing to become rich. I think of my father, who has played the lottery every week for thirty years, always using the same six numbers, without ever winning anything significant. Would you call that manifestation, even though hoping for a big lottery win is completely unrealistic?"

"Absolutely. He shouldn't stop, because imagine what it would do to him if he didn't fill out his lottery ticket once, and his six numbers were drawn that time!"

"That would be the real catastrophe", Phil laughs.

## Conversation with a Theologian

"By the way, you recently told me you'd like to discuss some topics that interest you with a theologian. I thought of Sabine Kramer from the Inselspital pastoral care team. You might even know her..."

"Hmm, no, the name doesn't ring a bell. I didn't know you had several theologians. I once had a visit from a pastor, I've forgotten his name, who introduced himself as a patient caregiver. A nice person, but visibly disappointed when I explained that I don't believe in a 'God in Heaven' to whom I can pray."

"He probably took that as a rejection", Phil smiles. "Our theologians are used to that and don't want to impose on anyone. But if you'd like, I'd be happy to introduce you to Sabine."

A week later, Beat is waiting in the cafeteria at the same table where he's had many conversations with Phil, for Sabine Kramer. He sees a woman, about fifty-five years old and slim, approaching him. She introduces herself as Ms. Kramer and kindly asks, "And you're the man who is writing a book and is also interested in questions of faith, right?"

Beat immediately likes the woman. "Yes, thank you for taking the time to meet me. I don't know what Phil has told you about me, but he said you could answer certain questions from a theological perspective that interest me."

"I'm curious to hear what you want to know, but I must tell you that I can't speak for all theologians. Our team includes various faiths, and we often have different views. Phil told me you're a member of the Evangelical Reformed Church and that you have an inner compass that guides you in making important decisions. Is that correct?"

Beat is pleased that Ms. Kramer gets straight to the point. He feels he can talk to her about everything he's read in thousands of pages about the law of attraction and conscious manifestation, and he shares how he left the free church as a young man and embraced Goddard's teachings. "That God isn't an unfathomable entity somewhere in the universe, but can be found within us, was the most important insight for me. Whenever I've met theologians since then, I've always wondered what their beliefs are, so

I'm asking you: Do you believe in a singular God, or can you imagine that something like divine power can be found everywhere in nature and within ourselves?"

Sabine listens attentively to Beat's speech without interrupting. Her expression reveals neither approval nor disapproval. "I assume you've received various answers from theologians. You probably don't expect me to answer in one sentence and either tell you that you're right or that you're on the wrong track. You yourself are not entirely sure what to hold on to in matters of faith. Right?"

Sabine's response surprises and unsettles Beat. What does she mean by that? Why does she assume I don't know what to believe? Is she unsure of what to answer and trying to dodge or buy time? He tries not to sound annoyed as he asks the theologian why she thinks he's searching for the right faith.

"Well, I see you as a seeker; otherwise, you wouldn't have wanted this conversation. I appreciate when people engage with such questions as you do. To answer your two questions: Yes, I believe there is a divine power everywhere in nature, and thus also within us. But considering every person as a divine being is something I resist when I see what some people are capable of in a negative sense. You would need to explain more precisely what you mean by God dwelling within us. Also, what do you understand by the term divine?"

"I think of the goodness in people, the creative power given to us... What do you think? You used the term earlier..."

"I, like you, think of something good, something wonderfully beautiful. The question of whether there is a singular God, the creator of the vast universe that has existed forever, leads to philosophical considerations. We quickly reach the limits of our imagination. Can you explain eternity, something that has no beginning and no end?"

Beat shakes his head.

"Exactly", Sabine continues. "For us humans, everything must have a beginning and an end; anything else exceeds our imagination, including the concept of a God in Heaven. The Bible says you should not make an image of God. As you know, that is one of the Ten Commandments that Moses received from God on Mount Sinai. It does not say that Moses saw

God during this encounter. This is one of countless examples where the Bible, especially the Old Testament, can only be understood symbolically. You should not imagine God as some kind of being. Does that answer your question sufficiently?"

Beat's uncertainty about what to think of the theologian dissolves like water vapor in the Sahara. "I'm glad you see it that way."

"I hope you don't misunderstand me. I do not disagree with you when you quote Neville Goddard, who was also a theologian, and say that the divine presence is to be found within ourselves. I can fundamentally agree with that; there is a good core in every person. But to consider oneself as divine or even as God, I find problematic."

"I understand. Goddard was thinking of the goodness in people and the recognition of our creative power. According to the law of attraction, we can create anything we desire. You can open doors to a fulfilled and successful life if you align your consciousness with the subconscious. I have acted according to Goddard's law of attraction and can say today that I have led and continue to lead a fulfilled and successful life."

Sabine Kramer smiles and nods. "I believe you. I'm happy for you that you've found your way and are happy."

Beat feels slightly unsettled again. He had hoped, well, what exactly, that she would be impressed or astonished? Or that she would have questions? As the theologian doesn't continue speaking, he asks her opinion about Goddard's law of attraction.

"Yes, I know what you mean. And you surely know that many authors have taken up the topic and are very successful in marketing their books. *Find your flow, follow your heart's voice, the laws of winners,* and so on. What should I say about that? What do you expect from me?"

"Those who think positively attract positive things. This is even scientifically proven. I wonder why some theologians see it differently and dismiss these books as nonsense." Beat makes little effort to hide his displeasure.

"Stop!" Sabine interrupts Beat firmly. "It is known and partly scientifically proven that someone who exudes positivity reaps positivity. The opposite is also true: Those who are sullen or depressed absorb negative confirmations of their thinking like a dry sponge. Where have you experienced that some theologians deny this fact?"

"There was a recent show on Swiss television where a theologian spoke contemptuously about positive thinking. That greatly disappointed me because it contradicts everything I believe and have experienced in my life."

"Interesting. Did this theologian explain what was wrong with positive thinking?"

Beat feels caught off guard. "Well, I don't remember exactly what he said. But he claimed that manifesting and positive thinking were nonsense. So, I changed the channel because I didn't need to listen to that."

The theologian laughs briefly and clears her throat before answering. "Okay. Maybe he explained further. I think I need to clarify some things. Many of our patients with burnout and mental illnesses end up with us. We can treat these people medically; there are proven methods for that. But we also try to support them in ways that lead them out of their depression. That doesn't work for these people if we just hand them a bestseller and recommend following the author's good advice to become happy and successful. To heal someone, you need to understand the causes that led to the illness or severe suffering. We often refer burnout patients to psychiatrists and psychologists we trust. In rare cases – if patients explicitly request and I can arrange it – I take on the treatment as a trained psychologist."

"You studied both theology and psychology?"

"Yes, such a combination is not uncommon for so-called pastoral caregivers. Positive thinking and manifesting are important components in treating people with depression. This doesn't apply only to our patients but sometimes also to doctors or nurses at the hospital who are exhausted and burnt out. At the beginning of therapy, before we get to positive thinking, clients need to vent their frustrations and tell me about their problems. This is not easy for everyone, but it's important for me to understand their situation. Everything negative must be put on the table; we have to deal with it. Most clients are relieved to talk to someone who shows understanding and genuine interest in their problems. Can you relate to that?"

That sounds convincing. Beat can relate to that, but the conversation isn't going as he had hoped. Do we now have to talk about all the problems that make others unhappy? He thinks of Markus. Didn't he also have to unload his troubles first before I could offer him a constructive suggestion?

Sabine seems to read his thoughts and continues, "You might be a lucky person, leading a fulfilled life in prosperity and owing it to the law of positive radiation. You have always made the right decisions and have been spared severe depression. You should be proud of that."

"Thank you, Ms. Kramer, I am primarily grateful for it. And I thank you for your explanations. I am impressed by what you do. I understand that you first have to deal with the fate of your clients before you can influence someone with positive thoughts."

"That was nicely put. Recently, a bumblebee flew into my living room through a half-open window and couldn't find its way out. It kept crashing against the windowpane, unable to understand that this wasn't the way to freedom, even though it saw the sun and blue sky above. Only when I guided it from the closed window to the half-open one did it fly out and away. Almost always, there's a way out for people from a difficult situation, but they are often unable to recognize the direction they need to go to get back on solid ground. They are too focused on everything that weighs them down."

"That was well said. And you have confirmed to me that with the courage to adopt a positive attitude, it's almost always possible to give life new momentum. But I have one last question..."

"Please, ask. I have a bit more time." Sabine glances casually at her wristwatch.

"Do you believe in life after death?"

The theologian gives Beat a questioning look and seems to ponder. Finally, she says there is no proof of an afterlife, but she can't rule out the possibility of being reborn and starting a new life in another body. But that, too, is a question of faith that people have been asking for thousands of years. "In biblical belief, resurrection means transformation into a new life, not revival. Whether I consider it possible depends on whether I believe in the resurrection of our soul, which is immaterial, while our body turns to dust or ashes after death."

"As a pastoral caregiver, you must believe that every person has a soul, right?"

The theologian smiles and concludes, "You are right. Let me share something with you: Your friend Phil, as a neurologist and brain researcher, has dealt with a phenomenon that he has told me about and that I find remarkable. He has often observed that patients with severe dementia and Alzheimer's disease, whose brain cells are largely destroyed, suddenly speak clearly and understandably shortly before their death, as if they were fully conscious and rational. It's as if the spirit – you might call it the soul – of the dying person renews itself before leaving the body it has inhabited for a lifetime.

It is also well known that people with near-death experiences, like you, remember details they perceived during the operation, while the monitor showed that their heart had stopped beating, meaning the patient was briefly clinically dead. So, it is not at all far-fetched to believe that our soul continues to exist after our death. We could also imagine that it is not the soul that leaves us, but the body that leaves our soul when it dies. I think that's a good closing point", says the theologian, indicating that she wants to end the conversation.

They say goodbye warmly, and Beat's thoughts are already circling around the formulations he will record in his gratitude journal that evening.


## Spiritual Intelligence / The Art of Manifesting

During the next conversation with Phil, Beat seizes the opportunity to ask a question that has been on his mind for a long time: "As a neurologist, I've always wanted to ask you: Can intelligence be measured?"

### IQ

"Interesting question", Phil says. "It's not one that can be answered with a simple yes or no. You're probably thinking of the IQ, which is determined by an intelligence test. We use similar tests, for instance, with patients who have had a concussion or a traumatic brain injury. We also used this method to examine you. But primarily, such tests are used to assess memory function, and the main goal is not necessarily to determine the intelligence quotient but to determine the best possible treatment.

"There are also many methods to measure a person's IQ, including linguistic and mathematical abilities, logical thinking, and spatial understanding. You're probably familiar with these tests that have tasks to be completed within a certain timeframe."

Beat confirms: "Yes, I've taken several different IQ tests, many voluntarily and out of pure interest to see the results. I've come to the conclusion that the importance of IQ is often overestimated. What do you think about that?"

The professor smiles and agrees. "Here's a small example: Erwin, a friend of mine, is a mathematician and works for an insurance company. Recently, he had to evaluate job seekers who had taken a test. One of the applicants gave an incorrect answer to a simple task. The question was: What is the fourth number in a series with the values 2, 4, 8? Instead of 16, which was expected, he answered 10.

This surprised Erwin because the man had solved more complex problems correctly. When Erwin asked him why he had answered differently than expected, the man said he knew 16 was expected but 10 could also be correct, depending on the perspective on the series. For example, the first three numbers could be constants added to the following numbers. The man got the job."

*The simplest solution to a problem is not always the only correct one.*

"It's important to know that there is no scientifically accepted exact definition of intelligence. Depending on the age group, different criteria should be used for questions and evaluations", Phil adds.

"I'm glad you mentioned that", Beat says. "I have other questions on this topic that interest me, like emotional intelligence, EQ, and what you think of spiritual intelligence, SQ. Maybe we can talk about that next time."

"Sure, I look forward to our next conversation", Phil replies.


## EQ

As Beat prepares for his next conversation with Phil, he recalls the book "Emotional Intelligence" by Daniel Goleman, which Harry Holzheu had once suggested as a basis for the seminar "Emotional Selling." The motto was: If you can't smile, you won't make a sale.

What Goleman wrote in his bestseller in the 90s is still true today and will remain true in the future, Beat believes. To be successful, one must have the ability to perceive, understand, and influence one's own and others' emotions.

Human behavior is driven by both reason and emotions, which are closely linked. Emotions do not keep pace with accelerated societal changes and appear archaic. Anger leads to aggression, fear to flight or withdrawal, happiness to enthusiasm, surprise to curiosity, sadness to adaptation to loss and new orientation. This is human, has always been so, and will always be so.

*

Now, Beat sits across from Phil again, this time on the rooftop terrace because it's a warm and sunny day.

"I've also read Goleman's *Emotional Intelligence*", Phil explains. "He is a science journalist and refers to Professor Howard Gardner of Harvard School, whose book *Multiple Intelligences* is required reading for students in neurology and psychology. I fully agree with the statement that there is not just one type of intelligence but several types, not just linguistic and cognitive abilities and everything related to logical thinking. Just to name a few typical examples:
- *Musical-rhythmic intelligence,* the talent for making music and composing.
- *Visual-spatial intelligence,* the talent to grasp the structure of both large spaces and confined areas. A good qualification for pilots, sculptors, chess players, or architects.
- *Kinesthetic intelligence,* the ability to skillfully use individual body parts like hand, foot, or mouth; it is important for dancers, actors, athletes, but also for craftsmen and surgeons.
- *Social intelligence,* also called *interpersonal intelligence*. It refers to the ability to recognize and understand the unspoken motives, feelings, and intentions of others and to positively influence them. You can also summarize this under the term *empathy*. It is a good prerequisite for successfully dealing with people, for example, for parents with their children, and is important for everyone working in care professions."

"Thank you, Phil! I've taken notes. It would be nice if many people in other professions, especially politicians and those with leadership responsibilities, could take a cue from social intelligence."

Phil grins broadly, saying that's probably wishful thinking. "But you mentioned last week that you're particularly interested in *spiritual intelligence*. What do you understand by that?"

## SQ

"I read a book on this topic by Danah Zohar and Ian Marshall: *Connecting With Our Spiritual Intelligence*. Besides IQ and EQ, they propose a third Q. As I understand it, they mean the intelligence that helps us put our actions and our lives in a larger context of meaning. In other words, SQ is the foundation that makes both IQ and EQ effective. Humans are meant to find meaning and value in what they learn and do."

Phil nods in agreement. "Okay, I see why SQ interests you. The book by physicist Danah Zohar and psychiatrist Ian Marshall is based on the latest findings in brain research. Alongside explanations of scientific facts, they delve into different ways of thinking, religions, and life models, which is really exciting but also challenging to read. What impact did the book have on you?"

"You know I keep a kind of diary, my gratitude and success journal", Beat replies.

"In it, I direct my thoughts to living every moment with a harmonious feeling. This way, my life circumstances align as well.

Genius is our mental heritage, it's the gift of recognizing the essence in every situation. It's not reserved for a few chosen ones and doesn't need to be learned, like intuition, but one must remember who we are or who I am. Genius and intuition are the link between humans and the divine universal energy that everyone has within *themselves*.

In finding myself, I expand my horizon. I feel the effectiveness of the spiritual laws, and with my imagination, I recognize the all-encompassing order. Tesla's physical laws, based on the numbers 3, 6, and 9, point to this order. They are the key to the universe, and from them, power and energy manifest. You know our coordinate system, which allows orientation anywhere on Earth. I'll quickly sketch what I mean."

Beat quickly draws a circle and lines on an unused napkin and explains: "The number 9 is 3 squared, and 3 is the first prime number. The square is the encompassing space, or in this case, the full circle, which is 360 degrees. Space is defined by three dimensions, and from this principle, you always think in terms of thirds. This makes it clear why 360 degrees equals a full circle. Everything contained within can be spatially divided, such as the surface topology of our Earth into longitude and latitude. A compass always shows you exactly where you are on Earth."

"Alright, that's known", Phil interrupts, apparently not seeing where Beat is heading. "Tesla's physical laws are undisputed. Tesla was no fantasist but a recognized scientist and significantly contributed to the advancement of X-rays, neon lights, and high-power plants. But regarding your example: If you think of the circle not as the Earth but as the face of a clock with the numbers 3, 6, 9, and 12 instead of the cardinal directions, you can divide the temporal dimension by the same principle. A full rotation of the Earth takes 24 hours, a day, which closes the circle. You often talk about your inner compass. Does it work by the same principle?"

"In a way, it does. The physical compass operates based on magnetic forces invisible to us. My inner compass is based on my intuition and consciousness, which act like two magnetic poles: knowledge and understanding on one side, feeling and subconscious on the other."

*"Do you make decisions logically and rationally, or impulsively and emotionally?"*

"In my life, my compass has repeatedly ensured that I did or said the right thing at the right place and time. What I do now, I do consciously and consider right. This creates an energy field of absolute calm around me. I am in a flow, the circle closes, and in this calm, my intuition—my compass—can work."

"I understand", says Phil. "Many of our decisions are made spontaneously; there's no time to think long and enter a meditative state first. Does your compass also have an influence in such situations?"

"Of course, you make decisions every day without much thought or questioning, for example, in traffic or during sports competitions. Experience and rules are crucial in these cases, but emotions and intuitions also play a role. Call it driving intelligence, game intelligence, or physical intelligence."

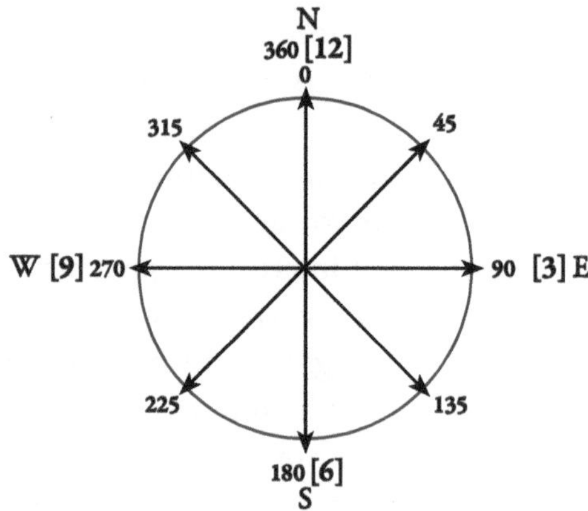



Beat now writes the terms *Stillness, Change—Security, Risk—Hope, Conviction—Ignorance, Life Experience* next to the direction and time indications in his compass drawing.

"When you face a decision and listen to your inner voice, you'll always get an answer and tend to lean in one direction or another emotionally, for example, choosing stillness or wanting to bring about change, relying on security, or being willing to take a risk. And you can also use other terms like *self-esteem* or *ethics* and *morality*."

"I know what you mean", Phil says. "The principle applies to you for short-term decisions where you have little or no time to act but also in situations where you need time to make the right decision. You consciously or unconsciously listen to your inner compass..."

"Yes. This can be impulsive depending on the situation or lead to a decision after longer consideration. When I take the time to calmly align myself with my being's energetic source, I receive impulses, words, flashes of thoughts, feelings, and sometimes even brief images and symbols that cannot be explained purely by reason. I believe in the effectiveness of my intuition and follow my heart's voice. I see my life goals and desires imaginatively and mentally take possession of them. I let my life compass guide me with serenity. My life has fundamentally changed since I began listening to and being guided by my life compass intuitively and mindfully. Living in harmony with my inner voice gives me everything I need for my spirit, soul, and human body, which I may inhabit for a limited earthly time. In such moments, I feel gratitude and joy."

"You once said that you regularly take a few minutes to meditate and listen to your inner compass in absolute calm. Do you still do that?"

"Yes, it's a kind of ritual, and I do it often and out of conviction because I feel the positive energy it gives me. Often, I watch one of Tepperwein's videos on deep relaxation. They offer tips and suggestions on how to consciously slow down life."

"That reminds me of Emile Coué", says Phil. "He was one of the founders of autosuggestion at the end of the nineteenth and the beginning of the twentieth century, and he inadvertently contributed to the flood of literature on manifesting and suggesting how to achieve everything you want."

## Conscious Autosuggestion

"You've studied autosuggestion? That's surprising", says Beat. "I didn't know you, as a scientist, were interested in such topics."

"Of course, as a neurologist, this subject is especially interesting to me", Phil explains with a grin. "By the way, Coué was a pharmacist in Troyes, a medium-sized town in France. Modern medical or psychology students hardly know about him, although his methods are becoming increasingly important in medical-psychological research. Perhaps it's because Coué's methods are incredibly simple; anyone can use them without studying complicated theories."

"You're still talking about autosuggestion. For me, the term is synonymous with affirmation."

"Yes, in a sense", Phil agrees. "Linguistically, affirmation means the approval or confirmation of a statement or claim. In esotericism and spiritual practices like mantra-like praying, affirmation is understood as a positive statement. Affirmations are also sometimes used as a technique in the treatment of mental disorders, in the sense of autosuggestion, as practiced by Coué."

"How did a pharmacist come up with this? Isn't he supposed to just sell medication?" Beat wonders.

"Let me briefly summarize what I've read about him: Emile Coué studied pharmacy and then opened a small pharmacy in his hometown. One day, he had a key experience: A man entered the pharmacy and demanded a prescription-only medication but couldn't provide a prescription. Despite the pharmacist's explanations that he had to adhere to legal regulations and couldn't give the medication without a prescription, the seriously ill man insisted. Coué had an idea: He pretended to comply, filled a bottle with distilled water in the back room, and gave the man the 'medicine' with precise instructions on how to take it and how it would work. A week later, the man returned, completely healed, and thanked Coué."

"Nice story", says Beat. "The placebo effect. Does that also fall under autosuggestion?"

"Well, it's certainly a form of suggestion. But the story didn't end there. Coué's research interest in psychology and hypnosis was sparked. He recognized the importance of suggestion,  hypnosis without hypnotic sleep, for example, and called it *self-hypnosis* or *positive autosuggestion*. Increasingly, people came to Coué not just for medicine but to talk to him and seek his advice. Gradually, the rumor spread in Troyes that Maître Coué was performing real miracles."

"Like the miracle healers in Appenzell or Isaac of Uluru, who heals Aborigines in the Australian outback", says Beat with a smile.

"Don't forget that Coué studied pharmacy and didn't see himself as a healer. He remained modest and didn't seek to capitalize on his knowledge. He always emphasized that he didn't deserve the credit when someone was healed—he was just helping people to heal themselves. As more and more spectacular healings occurred, he soon couldn't accommodate all the people seeking help in his pharmacy. So, he began holding his own events to conduct suggestion treatments and teach people how to use autosuggestion. He considered it proven that the subconscious played an important role in organic diseases and that conscious suggestion could fundamentally alleviate or even cure any disease.

At the beginning of the twentieth century, he quit his pharmacy career and founded the first Coué Institute in Nancy."

"What did his autosuggestion treatments look like?"

"Coué knew that imagination is stronger than willpower. 'It's not the will that drives our actions, but imagination' was his famous quote."

*With willpower alone, you achieve nothing; with imagination, everything!*

"That's actually in line with my way of thinking", Beat remarks. "Basically, this thesis has something in common with the law of attraction."

"That's true", Phil confirms. "Coué recognized an important characteristic of our subconscious: its incredible receptivity. It absorbs everything we hear, see, smell, and feel. Neurological theories suggest that consciousness and subconsciousness are reflected in the structure of our brain. It consists of two halves, the hemispheres, connected by nerve fibers that communicate with each other. Anatomically, these two hemispheres are almost identical. Today we know they have fundamentally different functions: The left hemisphere works logically and analytically, governed by reason, responsible for language, mathematics, and spatial orientation. The right hemisphere works intuitively and creatively. It's responsible for creativity, emotions, body language, and aesthetics. The subconscious stores everything and does what it's told. You could also call it naive, as it's not governed by reason."

"Does that mean it's easy to influence?"

"Exactly! Suggestion is influence. It's unsettling to think that someone else could suggest something to you and influence your behavior. When adults tell a child they're stupid or ugly, it creates a lasting negative self-image. Coué differentiated between suggestion and autosuggestion. For suggestion to be effective, it must turn into autosuggestion in the person being influenced."

"This can be positive or negative—depending on the intentions of the suggestor. How should one react when they see through bad intentions?"

Phil does what he always does when he considers how to explain a complex thought to his counterpart: He takes off his glasses and thoughtfully cleans the lenses. "Well, you first need to recognize the suggestor's intention, and for that, you need your mind, your consciousness. An entire industry thrives on suggestion: the advertising industry. As a former sales director of a large corporation, you're well acquainted with the tools of product advertisers."

"True!" replies Beat. "Even in large shopping centers where background music plays, it's usually certain music frequencies that encourage shopping. They call them binaural beats. They're supposed to improve sleep, attention, and memory, as well as reduce stress, pain, and anxiety. I've been interested in them for a few years and observe what happens to me, for example, with music for deep relaxation on *YouTube*."

"Interesting", says the neurologist. "Those must be very pleasant and soothing sounds. Unfortunately, suggestion can also be used abusively. Although humans are not robots but thinking beings, it still surprises me how successful fundamentalist religious leaders or populist politicians—let alone dictators—are in some countries.

But back to Coué. Of course, he knew that autosuggestion was a dangerous tool. Indeed, many diseases and most mental problems result from unconscious, i.e., negative, suggestion. There's no need to panic about it, because advertising is an unavoidable everyday phenomenon. Jealousy, envy, and schadenfreude are human traits we have to live with. We can only try to handle them as best as possible. Trust in oneself is important, so suggestion turns into conscious, positive autosuggestion."

Beat smiles: "Now you sound like an esoteric guru! Even *Neville Goddard*, with his law of attraction, believed that positive thoughts create positive outcomes. *Kurt Tepperwein* argues similarly, and *Bodo Schäfer* preaches the same."

"Alright, agreed! Maybe we're going in circles. Goddard and Coué were, without wanting to be, role models for institutions and many authors who teach autogenic training and positive thinking or recommend them in countless books.

The autosuggestion treatment based on Coué's model—coming back to your question—is very simple: If you feel stomach pain, you tell your subconscious that you feel better every day. You have to say it several times a day, without thinking about it. The crazy thing is: As a scientist, I have to admit from personal experience that it works. By the same principle, he developed magic formulas against insomnia, physical and mental ailments. Coué must be distinguished from authors who promise material wealth if you just manifest daily and firmly believe you're already on the way to becoming a millionaire."

"Wow! I don't know what your colleagues would say about that, but I like your open attitude toward autosuggestion."

"Don't worry about my colleagues! If you've never heard of surgical procedures where the patient undergoes an operation without anesthesia: It's increasingly practiced successfully with conscious autosuggestion and self-affirmation. Of course, only with professional guidance and all necessary safety measures to continue the operation conventionally if the patient signals they're in pain."


## Visions Are Needed

Markus Hofmann and Beat meet in a cafeteria in Bern. Beat had wanted to know how Markus was doing in his role as a new employee at the Federal Office for Economic Affairs, Education, and Research and was pleased that his old acquaintance was immediately available for a conversation. Markus doesn't seem like someone who battled deep depression a few months ago. After brief small talk, he begins to speak calmly: "I'm eternally grateful to you for helping me out of that low. It was a terrible situation; I felt like a hamster in a wheel before it knocked me down. Today, I'm doing well. The work at the WBF is demanding but exciting and fun."

Markus talks about his first experiences in his new professional environment and then says that he's had a lot of time to think about himself, his life, and today's society. "You know, I now see more clearly how our system works, and some things worry me."

"Worry you? I thought no one had to worry about you anymore", Beat says in surprise.

"No, it's not about me personally, but about our system. Specifically, the monetary system and our economy."

"Tell me more!"

"I'll start with an example. Before I emigrated to India 35 years ago, I paid 900 francs rent for a two-and-a-half-room apartment in Zurich. Today, I pay 2 700 francs for a comparable apartment in the city center. After deducting all fixed costs, I had about 2000 francs left for living 35 years ago. My last salary as a bank employee two years ago was about twice as high as 35 years ago, but I had even less than 2 000 francs left for living.

The difference is that the prices for food, drinks, clothes, communication, and so on have skyrocketed over the years. A hundred francs are still a hundred francs, as printed on the bill, but they no longer have nearly the same value as 35 years ago."

"And that worries you...?"

"As I said, I'm fine. Inflation in Switzerland is still bearable, but the collapse of Credit Suisse has significantly damaged public trust in our banks. How secure are our investments? Who determines the value of the money in circulation?

The money supply, for explanation, the money in circulation, is limited. Commercial banks get their money from the central or national bank. They lend this money with interest to the economy and private individuals and thus record their profits. That means, by granting loans or mortgages to businesses and individuals, the bank makes money. Based on debt interest."

"Yes, agreed. But that's just how our system works."

"Exactly. But something is being forgotten: the question of what our money is worth. You're surely familiar with the fall of the Roman Empire, aren't you?"

"Yes", laughs Beat, surprised. "But what did that have to do with the value of money?"

"A lot. The denarius was originally a 4.5-gram silver coin and remained unchanged for centuries. Then base metals like copper were mixed with the silver, but the coin kept the same weight. From emperor to emperor, more copper was added to the denarius. By 300 AD, the silver content was down to five percent, and soon after, the denarius was practically worthless. The result was hyperinflation, and massive war costs demanded more and more money. Money that no longer had value."

"So, in the end, the denarius had only symbolic value", concludes Beat. "What about today's currencies?"

"Now it gets interesting", says Markus. "In 1971, US President Nixon decided to suspend the dollar's convertibility into gold. For the first time in history, all major world currencies were freed from the gold standard. When Switzerland joined the International Monetary Fund (IMF) in 1992, it also abandoned the gold standard for the Swiss franc."

"And that means...?"

"Initially, there was a dramatic devaluation of the dollar. In the 1960s, it cost over four Swiss francs; today, it's 90 cents. Today, central banks determine the value of a currency based on the money supply in circulation and measured by the gross domestic product of a country. Therefore, money and currency are two different things. The US national debt exceeds 30 trillion dollars, and the Swiss National Bank sits on a debt mountain of 120 billion francs, with a rising tendency. The EU is in a debt crisis, and solutions are only discussed but not really tackled."

"What needs to happen to avoid a huge crash?"

"You know, I've often thought of you and how you got me out of a negative spiral of thinking. This time, it's not about me or individuals needing an intuitive and positive push to get out of depression. It's about changing a system that impoverishes and sickens many people, similar to the Monopoly game. The game ends only when the winner is determined, or all other players are bankrupt. Only the bank never goes bankrupt; it can always issue new bills, i.e., grant loans. We live in a time of collapse and the dawn of a new era. Wealth is defined purely materialistically through more possessions, more consumption, and growth, which leads to more environmental destruction. A kind of new testament needs to be written, defining wealth not by the bank balance."

"Phew, I hope you don't seriously expect me to come up with a magic formula to save the world now."

Markus shakes his head. "No, that wasn't the intention. Individuals can't do anything against the banking and financial system and the devaluation of money. Also, developing and implementing new thinking models is a long process. It requires new awareness and visions. I would already consider it a huge progress if decision-makers from politics and business didn't short-sightedly politicize and act against each other out of self-interest but were committed to working together to prevent the plundering of the planet's last resources."

Beat is amazed and impressed by how much Markus has developed in recent months from an apathetic loser to someone more concerned about the environment than himself. "A noble wish", he says. "But I like the thought that you and your team are open to new visions. Are you a kind of think tank where experts and representatives from politics and business talk to each other?"

"It's heading in that direction. Of course, we must think globally, and as soon as economic and political interests of a country come into play, it gets complicated. We're looking for consensus first. There are various approaches to solutions being tested here and there, such as the introduction of a universal basic income or blockchain technology, which relies on a decentralized protocol for transactions that is fraud-proof. The latter consumes an enormous amount of energy and is therefore controversial. Whether and how something new proves itself will be shown by the future. I just wanted to make you understand what we deal with at the WBF and what worries us. I must not take it personally, and I often remember your advice: There is so much positive to build on. You just have to tackle it!"

Beat is relieved that Markus finds his work exciting and enjoys his new job, which challenges him.

# Thoughts on the Future

On the Earth's surface, you can orient yourself using a compass. The magnetic needle of the compass aligns with the Earth's poles and shows you the direction you are heading.

Beat has often intuitively consulted his imaginary inner compass when he had to make important decisions. His recent encounter with Markus, who is more concerned about the state of our Earth than about himself, has touched him.

Wealth is defined materialistically by more possessions, more consumption, and consequently more environmental destruction, Markus had said, adding that a new testament should be written that does not reduce wealth to a bank balance.

My life has developed positively, Beat thinks. My inner compass, which also works according to the law of attraction, has often caused me to make good decisions. My visions have been fulfilled through manifestation and affirmation.

An important point of attraction for me was wealth, he knows, and finds nothing wrong with that. He has reached at least the second-highest level of Maslow's hierarchy of needs, the satisfaction of individual needs. He leads a comfortable life, is married to a lovely wife, enjoys his three adult children and four grandchildren, and has good friends. For this, he is grateful. He also considers the highest level, self-actualization, to be achieved, but knows that he still sets new goals. Maybe I will only stop having higher goals in old age, he thinks. Now I am writing a book and would be happy if readers find one or two positive thoughts in it and are inspired to try communicating with their inner compass.

Markus has made him aware that there are problems on our planet that a single person cannot solve. Wars, human rights violations, environmental damage, national debt, and large movements of refugees are global realities that affect us all indirectly or directly.

Thinking positively does not mean ignoring or downplaying problems but also perceiving the positive. Every person has their own goals and possibilities, depending on gender, age, origin, education, health, family, and friends. In our personal environment, we can make a difference. We can influence what happens to us.


## Quanta

When we hear the term "quanta", we inevitably think of quantum physics and Einstein's theory of relativity or the term "quantum leap", which in everyday language means a significant advancement achieved in a very short time. In Latin, "quantum" means something large, measurable, or "quantifiable."

Beat was interested in quantum physics and quantum waves. He came across astonishing explanations about the borderline between the quantum world and the world of classical physics. Electronic or photonic components leave the framework of previously known fundamental laws of physics (Max Planck Institute research report, 2020).

The quantum world is bizarre. All particles behave uniformly like waves when isolated from their surroundings. But when a quantum particle comes into contact with its surroundings, quantum leaps can disrupt and scramble the previously calculable process. Quantum leaps occur randomly; they are events and therefore have a temporal direction, distinguishing the future from the past.

In the world of quantum waves, resonance is crucial, meaning being in harmony with each other or with something that vibrates on the same frequency. Energy waves that a person sends out inevitably respond to energy that vibrates similarly or the same.

*Quantum objects behave as if they have a mind.*


## Einstein

The world-famous physicist and visionary Albert Einstein also left his mark in Bern: the unique Einstein Museum, the Einstein Lectures at the University of Bern, and the Einstein House on Kramgasse, where he lived from

1903 to 1905. The genius of the century is also immortalized as a statue on benches at four locations in the city, such as at the University of Bern, where Beat has visited several times and taken selfies with the sculpture. Each time, Beat wonders how Einstein came to the groundbreaking insights over a hundred years ago that form the basis of today's advanced technology in astronomy and atomic and quantum sciences.

Beat has read a lot about Einstein and studied his biography. The future developer of the theory of relativity discovered mysterious forces affecting the compass needle as a boy. This inspired him to find out more about invisible energies. Einstein was more than a famous scientist. He became a legend in his lifetime and is now a myth.

During a technical discussion with his Danish physicist colleague Niels Bohr and the German Max Born, Einstein summarized his rejection of atomic physics in three legendary words: "God does not play dice!"

Einstein always spoke as a physicist and cosmologist, not as a theologian. In his biographical sketches, there is an interesting note:

*"Science without religion is lame, religion without science is blind."*

Beat did not want to delve into the difficult-to-understand theories of Albert Einstein or the complex scientific explanations of Isaac Newton on quantum mechanics, but while browsing specialist literature, he came across the interesting books Quantum Economy by Anders Indset and Quantum Philosophy by Ulrich Warnke. Both are easy to read, Beat thought, and they encourage reflection on developments that will concern us all greatly in the future.

## Quantum Economy

In his book, which appeared on the top ranks of the Spiegel bestseller list in 2019, Norwegian author Anders Indset deals with gigantic quantum computers, empathetic robots, and artificial intelligences. These would have fundamental impacts on our future, our economic system, your job, and your life, Indset claims.

At the beginning of his book, the author reminds us of the beheading of Louis XVI in 1792 and the associated downfall of the monarchy in France. Before the last Louis, fifteen other kings of the same name had sat on the throne, making a radical system change overdue. During feudalism, nobles received incomes without having to provide services. The Catholic clergy was privileged in the second estate, while everyone else, the actual people, belonged to the third estate. Even teachers, philosophers, and inventors were as underprivileged as the hungry, illiterate peasants and craftsmen. The "Louis model" was no longer compatible with the real needs of a large majority and had to be destroyed. The revolutionaries' slogan and Enlightenment thinkers like Voltaire asserted that all people have the same rights. In some countries like Great Britain or Sweden, the royal houses have survived but now serve only as decoration and symbolic representatives of the respective nation.

Indset compares the downfall of the Ancien Régime to the situation we find ourselves in today: Again, power and wealth are in the hands of a very small privileged group of fewer than a hundred people who own as much wealth as the poorer half of the world's population, almost four billion people. The author does not blame capitalism for this imbalance but advocates for developing the economy so that the capitalist engine is not stalled but can be used for fairer distribution.

*Quantum Economy is based on the understanding that everything is interconnected: We need to relearn to view the economy, society, and ecology holistically.*

Indset does not believe that a happier society will automatically emerge if everyone just follows the compass of their self-interest. In the following three hundred pages, the author explains his ideas of a quantum economy, focusing particularly on the development and possibilities of artificial intelligence.

Indset differentiates between "weak and strong AI": Weak AI are programs for solving specific application problems, examples being facial recognition and navigation systems. Strong AI, on the other hand, is general intelligence that is equal to or superior to human intelligence. A machine equipped with general intelligence (AGI) would be capable of logical thinking, learning from mistakes, making decisions, communicating in natural languages, and using all these abilities in a coordinated manner to achieve its goals, similar to how we think but incomparably faster and more precisely. Prototypes of AGI have already been developed.

These explanations made Beat reflective. He considers Indset's appeal that we must now ask ourselves whether we will control AI or whether AI will control us as justified.


## Quantum Philosophy

*Ulrich Warnke,* who studied biology, physics, geography, and education and has been living in retirement in Saarland since 2010, wrote the book Quantum Philosophy and Interworld as a guide for a completely new life task, through which we are to become "powerful actors of the universe" from spectators.

The book is a journey into the realm of the continuously active, intelligent, yet largely undiscovered quantum consciousness. Here, it becomes apparent that the waves of matter are "immaterial probabilities" at their core. The same applies to the waves of the mind, which move our thoughts, emotions, and intuitions. What is the Interworld?

This question occupied Beat, and he found explanations: Warnke says that the only immutable, concretely graspable reality is not the world of matter but what he calls the Interworld. In it, he finds all ideas and forms with which we can recognize our reality – like pure consciousness. Without consciousness, there would be no matter for us.

The material body is merely a temporary vessel for spirit and soul, says Warnke, asking what kind of vessel it is that is available to us for decades. What is the nature of its matter, he asks, referring to the great religions of humanity, all of which assume an afterlife. Body matter would turn to ashes and dust after death and decay, but not spirit and soul. According to Warnke, they are part of the Interworld.

A comforting thought, Beat finds and continues reading:

The mind can create an outer world, just as a writer imagines a world that exists only in his head. In everyday life, this happens completely unconsciously without us even noticing it. As long as we adhere to a one-sided, purely material concept of reality, the true nature of the world remains hidden from us.

In everyday life, we orient ourselves by seeing, smelling, tasting, and touching. This is necessary because our five senses guarantee our survival, ensure we get food, and do everything to create ideal living conditions for our bodies. Gradually, humans discovered that they could harness other energies, such as electromagnetic energy. Eventually, they reached the building blocks of matter, the atoms. As is well known, atoms consist of an atomic shell, electrons, and a nucleus composed of protons and neutrons. Atoms are directed by forces that only act over short distances, known in physics as strong and weak forces. Everything that makes up our everyday world, everything we perceive with our senses, cars and airplanes, villages and cities, is based on these fundamental forces.

But atoms alone cannot explain our feelings and imagination. Why are we capable of believing and thus changing our reality? For a long time, these questions were approached through philosophical considerations or exact natural sciences. The essence was not reached. Quantum philosophy has changed that. We recognize that humans – like the entire universe – do not only live in the everyday world of fundamental forces but even predominantly in a completely different world: the world of consciousness.

Alright, I will think about this calmly, Beat decides. He flips through the book and finds a section on "Multiple Personalities" at the back:

Everyone can slip into different personalities in their imagination. Good actors master this transformation perfectly. But you don't have to be an actor to know the power of an imaginary role. If we intend to give a speech before an audience, it can only succeed if our self-image matches, if our personality adopts the appropriate role. Then we do not act but bring forth a person within us that we have always been, because we could be – nothing else is the sea of possibilities that the Interworld offers us daily.

Beat finishes reading the comprehensive book and concludes that it would be exciting to discuss Warnke's theories and Indset's book Quantum Economy with Phil, which deals with future changes that will undoubtedly concern us all. More and more often, the media writes about the turning point we are currently and will be facing in the near future.

*Which direction your inner compass points to and whether you will follow it will be shown by the future.*

# Conclusion / Resumee

As Beat reflects on the ideas of Einstein, Indset, and Warnke, he realizes that they all point to the same fundamental truth: that we are all interconnected and that our actions have consequences that ripple through the fabric of reality. Whether we are talking about the environmental impact of our economic system, the implications of quantum physics for our understanding of the universe, or the need for a new consciousness that recognizes our interconnectedness, the message is clear: we are all part of a larger whole, and our actions matter.

Beat feels inspired by these ideas and resolves to live his life in a way that is aligned with this deeper understanding of reality. He knows that he cannot solve all the world's problems single-handedly, but he also knows that he can make a difference in his own sphere of influence. By living with awareness and compassion, by making choices that are in harmony with the greater good, he can contribute to the ongoing evolution of consciousness and help to create a better world for future generations.

As he gazes out at the stars on a clear night, Beat feels a sense of awe and wonder at the beauty and complexity of the universe. He knows that there is still much that he does not understand, but he also knows that he is part of something greater than himself. And in that knowledge, he finds peace and purpose.

In which direction your inner compass points and whether you will follow it, the future will show.

# Postscript

## Dear reader

You have reached the end of the book "Your Compass". There is not much more to be written about the author and his life. His life is interwoven in this story. From the age of 50, I was often asked what I would do as a retiree. The answer was very simple, I would continue to travel the world, discover other cultures, and want to write a book. You have now read the book and noticed that it is not a normal biography, although all the most important events happened as it has been told.

At the beginning of writing, I, as an inexperienced author, wondered where to start. Birth, childhood, schools, profession, parents, hobbies, and so on? No, that's boring! I received advice from an author to start right away with the cardiac arrest on June 21, 2019, in Ticino. At first, this was unthinkable for me. This event would be too negative a start, I told myself. But while writing, all the elements that could be associated with it intuitively emerged step by step. I came to the realization that it is not wrong sometimes not to know where the journey will lead, without already knowing the way exactly. The only thing that matters, no matter where you are in your life right now, is to proceed lovingly and calmly, with a vision for yourself. I became aware that my inner compass of life would guide me on the way to write the book. Writing the book, being in the "flow," was pure psychotherapy, contemplation, and self-reflection for me.

Start by accompanying yourself with understanding and love on your way. So be loving and patient with yourself on your further journey and respect that you have made this decision. You will find out who you really are. It takes a bit of courage to question one's own self-image and worldview. Often we not only encounter criticism and misunderstanding from ourselves but also from our environment. Trust your compass, the voice within you that believes in you and knows that you will find and follow your path.

You, dear reader, have planted a golden seed in your heart with the knowledge and experiences from this book. With every positive thought, with every wonderful imagination, and with every loving word to yourself, this little seed grows, becoming a strong tree whose fruits you will reap and under whose shade you can rest. Follow your dreams and desires. It is part of human nature to have desires and set goals. There is no end goal in life, our consciousness is timeless and eternal, residing in the body to experience various experiences on Earth. All that exists is this moment, the NOW! This moment is perfect, it contains everything and shapes your future. Everything you need is already within you.

The book begins with the near-death experience and deals with theological and philosophical questions. One reason for writing this book was to find out what answers and insights I would gain from experiences beyond death and the return to life.

In conversations with theologians and neurologists, and in literature from books that address the meaning of our existence on Earth, I tried to incorporate comparative scientific findings from quantum physics, medicine, neurology, theology, and philosophy.

Where is the Bible right, how is it to be understood, literally or symbolically? How and where does philosophy relativize things that revelations from history have left us?

We had to realize that in our sacred texts, poetry and truth often lie closely together, and that the transmitted word - the Logos - does not always provide reliable information about the true connections of life. We learned how deceptive religions can be, how uncertain their statements can be at times, but also how deep wisdom is sometimes hidden in them. Philosophy, on the other hand, offers us a multitude of interpretations that can only be delimited and ordered by the filter of wisdom from the afterlife.

The story in the compass book can lead to a new perspective, in which questions about where, why, and where to in my life are interwoven. The new perspective is primarily drawn from the old wisdom, intertwined with new technologies in quantum physics, neurology, psychology, and artificial intelligence. We ventured into levels of consciousness that provide us with new perspectives, new truths, and new insights. One of the most important insights is to understand how much we are all created from a unit of energy. Today it is recognized that we are not just one world, we are an organism, a spiritual entity, and intimately connected to each other.

We see matter with different eyes. We will increasingly recognize our material world as a virtual product of our psychic presence, because as long as we do not free ourselves from the prison of our materialistic worldview, there will be no true freedom of the mind.

The spark of God's energy lives in every human being, even in the atheist. So which religion can claim to be the only saving one? Which faith tradition can claim to be the only one that leads to God? Whoever is truly seeking will also find the truth. After the transition to the afterlife, we finally encounter our own SELF, and we recognize who we really were and are: eternal perfect being in a wonderful body, on Earth to gain experiences. Even the famous Greek philosopher Plato recognized that the body is merely a useful serving object. It submits to the soul/spirit in humans. The soul makes use of the body. With its help, it participates in the material world. The body is its tool for sensual experience. Accordingly, death is neither a punishment nor an evil for Plato, but the liberation from the captivity of human limitation and spiritual narrowness. Plato reversed the conditions by saying: Who knows if life is only death, dying, on the other hand, life?

We are now in a great global shift of consciousness, and every human being can feel it and is called upon to come into their "divine power," to awaken to themselves. I also wrote the book "Your Compass" to address you with intuition and impulses, as I have experienced them, to be guided on the path to true creative power. Because it is also your intuition that guides you like a compass in this turbulent time.

I bless you. You are a human energy field and always radiate what you are. Your consciousness continuously creates, consciously or unconsciously, your reality. Focus your attention with your thoughts always on living in harmony with a good feeling with yourself in every moment, and your life circumstances will shape themselves fittingly for you.

I wish you courage to intuitively take the step from the EGO mind to the SELF and to be able to do it mentally. You are perfect eternal BEING and with your awakening to yourself, you will discover the divine power within you, as described by all prophets, Buddha, and Christ in the Bible. Our body is also our temple, in which God resides.

By immediately understanding what is, was, and will be, you transcend the limits of the mind and reach perfect thinking and feeling. The left logical hemisphere of the brain will then give way to the right emotional hemisphere and serve where your intuition is and works.


## Finally, a few tips for activating your inner compass

Imagination

Take a few minutes each day to visualize your goals and desired outcomes. Imagine them as vividly as possible. You see, hear and feel what it triggers in you.

Mental rehearsal: Practice scenarios in your head in which you achieved your goals. This mental rehearsal prepares your brain for success in real life. Feel like you have achieved what you wanted and accept it gratefully. This is the secret of visualization.


Consciousness

Participate in a mindfulness exercise to increase your awareness of the present moment. Remain calmly in the flow state. This can be achieved through meditation, deep breathing, or simply being fully present in your daily activities.


Self reflection

Regularly reflect on your thoughts, feelings and actions. Take notes, journaling can be a helpful tool as it allows you to explore your inner world and recognize patterns.

Affirmations

Positive Statements: Create a positive affirmation that reflects your goals and desires. Examples: "I am capable of achieving my dreams." "I deserve success and happiness." and "I trust my inner guidance."

Repetition: Repeat your affirmations daily, preferably in front of a mirror. Consistency is key because repeated exposure helps your brain solidify these positive statements.

Activate your inner compass

Set intentions: Start the day by setting clear intentions. Decide what you want to achieve and focus your energy on those goals.

Listen to your intuition: Pay attention to your positive feelings and intuitive impulses. Your inner compass often communicates through subtle feelings and thoughts.

Action: Take first steps that are consistent with your goals and values. Make sure your daily activities reflect your true desires and aspirations. By integrating imagination, awareness and affirmations into your everyday life, you can effectively activate your inner compass and move closer to fulfilling your desires.

Being in harmony with your inner compass, setting new goals and realizing your wishes cannot be achieved overnight. In my next book, let's call it *Compass Two*, I will discuss these topics in more detail.

I wish you courage, joy, love, and harmony when crossing over with intuition into the new state of consciousness.

*Warm regards, Beat*

# Name Index

*The book "Your Compass" was translated from German to English using OpenAI ChatGPT. The author and the publisher decided to retain the English as written by the artificial intelligence. This decision was particularly fitting, given that the themes of artificial intelligence and future topics are discussed in this autobiographical non-fiction novel.*

*Beat and Werner wish you much fun and enjoyment.*